SIMON SAYS

a novel

MARGARET RITTER

SIMON SAYS A NOVEL

BOSTON • TORONTO

LITTLE, BROWN AND COMPANY

LIBRARY OF CONGRESS CATALOG CARD NO. 66–20804

FIRST EDITION

Published simultaneously in Canada
by Little, Brown & Company (Canada) Limited

PRINTED IN THE UNITED STATES OF AMERICA

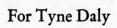

For Tyne Daly

For Tyne Daly

THE LONG PROLOGUE

1

IT was just before tea, on Maundy Thursday, when I decided to become an actress. The spring holiday had begun and I had been set free from Miss Rose's School for Young Ladies for a fortnight, a fortnight in which I must get used to the idea that I was not going to graduate if I did not cram enough French verbs to pass the finals.

"I'm afraid, my dear . . ." Miss Rose had said in her most painful voice, "there will be no way to pass you out as a graduating senior, without a really high mark in the French final."

It was clearly impossible. I could not conjugate. I tried but I could not.

Poor Miss Rose, how she hated blots on her escutcheon. She had never wanted to take me to begin with. Children of theatricals are so often flighty. Miss Rose had not founded her school for anything but the finishing of young gentlewomen and never again did she intend to accept the child of strolling players.

Of course the parents, Helen and Brandon, did not literally stroll from castle to castle giving performances in the courtyard, but they had, in their fashion, got about a good bit.

I sat in my room looking out over Central Park West and the end of winter. The great middle-class apartment in which

3

we lived was a pretense of spacious elegance, set on the wrong side of the park. I should never have supposed one could leave it by way of Miss Rose's. Helen's husband, Mr. Margolies, had arranged my commitment to Miss Rose's. He had been brought up a gentleman. It was just bad luck he had fallen into the pit of the theatre.

I shut the French grammar and laid it aside on the table, its covers never to be opened again by me. I decided to run away from the impossible. This was the finale of my childhood. The tyranny of adults was to be overthrown. I was not going to be like Helen, I was going to find someone to love for ever and ever and someone to love me and it was going to be the same someone for a lifetime. How wonderful, after all these years of emotional frostbite, to know at last I was going to be free.

Of course, I might not find my someone right away. I'd have to be prepared to wait a bit, and while I was waiting I'd have to work at something to secure my independence. There wasn't a lot I was fit to do. Machines broke down when I touched them and being a filing clerk was out because I didn't know the alphabet, so I chose acting.

Acting had the advantage of being the family trade. But best of all, how lovely, lovely to hide in someone else's identity while I found my own.

Since I knew in that instant that my future was to be the stage, I thought I ought to tell. It's no good knowing if you don't tell. Only by telling can one know if one's told the truth or a lie. Silence is a cove of fantasy, an illusion produced in the dark.

I ran down the wall-to-wall-carpeted halls to find Helen. Helen was in her study, all pink as Elizabeth Arden.

She reclined on her pink velvet chaise which was lit from a concealed fixture in a bath of surprise-pink light. Helen wore her cerise "at home" robe which hid her figure and flattered her neck.

4

She was being Elizabeth Barrett Browning studying a play script. It was set at the end of the chaise on a pink enameled music stand. Helen was farsighted. Her arms grew shorter every year but from where she sat far back in the chaise, she could read the script perfectly. She gazed upon it intently, orchestrating it in her mind's theatre.

Mr. Margolies said that the actor today must, more than ever before, realize himself as a part of the whole and fit himself into the orchestration of the entire work. Mr. Margolies was Helen's present husband, very round, very sincere. He thought the theatre was a religion and Helen one of its saints.

His real name was Herman but Helen had not liked that. She had changed it to Eric, which for some reason she found more suitable. I never called him anything but Mr. Margolies.

I really do not know what Mr. Margolies had done with himself before he married Helen. I gathered he had sat in the balcony from early childhood on, admiring the plays and the players. He had his own income but no talent for anything but serving at the altar. There had been an attempt, I believe, to edit a theatrical magazine, but he had not done anything since he married Helen but manage her affairs.

That's what he said. With a perfectly straight gaze, his two earnest, black eyes like plums in the Christmas pudding, he would sit and talk to total strangers about managing her affairs.

Not that Helen could have found much spare time for affairs because Mr. Margolies was always there beside her, living in the leftover light of her surprise-pink spot.

Helen looked very warm and protected in her pink womb. Helen is not pretty, but then stage women seldom are. Helen's very easy to caricature. Helen is all eyes, rosebud mouth and that mop of wild yellow hair.

It was clearly as impossible as the French verbs but I could not help wishing I could have seen Helen when she was young. Not known her, you understand but seen her — been a part of her audience. I should like to have seen her in *The Shrew* when she and Brandon first met and fell in love. I have seen the photographs, but they only show two second-drawer English actors in a 1937 coronation performance in the park.

Helen must have been adorable; the body slim, the hair really yellow, the eyes bright blue, the little mouth so pink — not a big raucous shrew, a small dainty shrew for dainties all are Kates. A Kate who fell in love with Petruchio the moment she clapped eye on him and would have him for her consolation as soon as he could win her.

Helen's acting game was never endurance. Helen's game was the place-shot that wore out her opponent. Her small, clear voice was formidable in use of pause and inflection. Her ability to remain in control infuriated the other actors and delighted her audience. She was the perfect Kate for Brandon.

Brandon was curly-black-haired, full-red-lipped, firm-fleshed and male. He was used to standing, stallion legs set wide apart, while women fell down before him, ran after and danced about him in delirious delight. Brandon's voice was an organ of sonorous, beautifully colored tones. Brandon's acting game was that tone. Oh, he could make a sound, when he wanted to.

He was thirty-nine that coronation summer and could not bear it. It was a lie he would not believe. Helen was thirty and yearning after a passion that would be truly grand.

Brandon had a perfectly good wife he'd had for donkey's years and a son of sixteen. Until Brandon met Helen, he had never considered giving them up or giving up women. Brandon led a very well-rounded life.

Helen had a chemist husband she had married one season

when she was nineteen, playing Rep in Manchester and the financial side of the theatre had looked chancy. Helen had driven the chemist before her to London when she had come to the West End. Helen had two little boys, a part-time nanny, a semi-detached villa in Ham, and a wild choking sensation when she thought what she might have had if she had waited a little longer.

Helen and Brandon never loved themselves or each other half as much again as they did that coronation summer. They were ready and ripe for each other. Edward had chosen his Simpson and they chose each other.

It was sticky, of course, a divorce takes longer than babies in England. They came to Hollywood to have me in exile just before the war began. The British colony there was sort of a celluloid Estoril. I was an August baby, a Leo, very good for the stage.

They made a film. Brandon became the rage, an American idea of the perfect English lover, cool in the drawing room and hot between the sheets. Helen was a flop. The camera did not treat her stage face very kindly.

Helen sulked. There were scenes over starlets. Helen insisted they go to New York and do a play. She had found a script she knew would be a hit because she had cried when she read it. It was about two people separated by the war in the first act, by death in the second, who find each other again in the third out in Ghostville, where they adopt a ghost orphan and muddle on down through eternity together. Brandon said it was a cross between *Peter Ibbetson* and *Smilin' Through*.

He was absolutely right but so was Helen. It ran two years on Broadway and toured a third. Through it all they did their war bit, selling bonds and serving doughnuts and being photographed at the Stage Door Canteen. They represented small, blitzed, brave England in America. They were the reverse of lend-lease.

Then one day the war was over, the play closed, and their golden weather was at an end. From '46 to '48 they waited for another play and rowed and blamed each other. Helen became more like the shrew of the first act and Brandon went back to women full time.

At last, exhausted, they got a divorce. Brandon got custody of Hollywood. Helen got Broadway, the straw-hat circuit and eventually Mr. Margolies as a fringe benefit.

I got to be held hostage by Helen and abandoned by Brandon, except when it suited Helen's purposes to send me off to see Brandon for state occasions such as her marriage to Mr. Margolies or her rehearsals.

These days Helen looked a little tired. She slowly turned the page of her playscript. Her brow was furrowed, her rosebud lips pouted. Helen did not understand the "new" theatre. It went one way and she another. Nothing in her being fitted her to play any of the characters. Poverty, rape, incest, torture, murder, riot — all her youth she had fought to get away from such common things. She had striven mightily to get onto the drawing room of the stage where she could dress well, speak well and be forever adorable.

After Brandon, Helen had tried a Shaw, in which she had passed for fair; an Ibsen that did not fare at all and a commercial comedy about a lady novelist and her efforts to marry off her too-young lover to her stepdaughter which had almost been amusing.

Then, when work did not come, would not come, and could not be coaxed, Mr. Margolies had said it was because the "new" theatre was too shoddy for a real artist to bother with.

This new play was to be a summer tryout on the straw-hat circuit and then come into New York if it looked promising. They were producing the "package" themselves. "Package" is a theatrical euphemism meaning "take me, take my production." Certainly no one else would produce it.

Mr. Margolies said he thought the play had solid Ibsen construction combined with the poetry of Williams and the insights of Inge. The play was about a mother, a daughter, a man and a mother's sacrifice. I was not sure what the mother's sacrifice was. I had not been asked to read the play.

If Helen minded playing the mother's part, she was going to have to lump it — forty-nine was forty-nine and would never be twenty again.

"Helen," I whispered softly. I meant to break my news about going on the stage gently. Sometimes just the tone of voice did wonders in conditioning Helen's responses. I spoke too softly. Helen did not hear me. She read on, her lips moving. An intellect Helen was not. Logic need look for no place in her lexicon but Helen should never be underestimated — she was capable of terrifying intuitions.

Dear Helen. The neck was crepe behind the choker of pearls framed in the ruffled lace. The eyes were fading blue, the eye shadow brighter than any sky. The hair was counterfeit. The silhouette was running toward stylish stout. And yet the old set of the head, the placement of the voice, the pause were just the way they must have been when she placed her hand beneath Petruchio's foot. No brown blotches on her hand then to show romance its foolish end.

"Helen," I said, as soft as kittens, "I'm going on the stage."

"There," Helen said not looking up, "you see, I was quite right to make you get your teeth straightened. You said it wasn't worth the effort, but you'll thank me for it. You'll see I can be right every now and again. Eyes used to be everything, now it's teeth."

Suddenly a small parenthesis of a frown formed between the eyes. The rosebud mouth puckered ominously.

"I suppose this is your father's doing."

"No," I said, "mine." Helen looked up, squinted at me for

9

a moment, and then satisfied I was telling the truth, sighed.

"You'll have to tell Brandon yourself, I don't want him blaming me. You know he never sent a penny for your teeth."

"No," I said, "I know he didn't."

"Don't you have a school holiday soon?"

"It began yesterday."

"Then go out to California and tell him your news." Helen brightened. "Yes, do go, I have the playwright coming here for rewrites and I can give him your room. Eric will get you a reservation on the plane."

"Thank you, Helen," I said. How familiar — being passed back and forth between the two of them.

Helen turned the page, her lips began to move and I went back to my room and began to pack.

2

BRANDON was in Palm Springs, resting. He lay beside his pool on an air cushion, hiding behind his dark glasses. There was a vodka and tonic nesting in his hand.

I had not expected Brandon to meet the plane. I had even wired ahead, "Do not meet plane," but I couldn't help looking about for him at the airport just in case he might be there. How I hated those vulnerable reflexes.

I took a very expensive taxi to his house. The thin young wife in Western pants gave me breakfast on the patio. I had had breakfast on the plane but I didn't communicate well enough with her to be able to say, "No, thank you." So I had breakfast again with the thin, young wife in the Western pants and her two adorable, plump babies.

She always wore skin-tight Western pants. I had had a fantasy once that she went to a ball with the pants on under her ball gown. Oh Freud, Oh Jung!

I made her nervous. It was not just that she was young enough to be Brandon's daughter that made her nervous, it was that Brandon was old enough to be my father. Even that didn't make her wild with nerves until she had to look at me and then at the two plump, adorable babies and admit to herself that they might have been Brandon's grandsons. Then she was absolutely stuck with the knowledge that Brandon was my father-figure, not hers.

The babies were sweet, two boys; two grown ones for Helen, two infants for Brandon and me in the middle along with that poor oaf Brandon had abandoned to marry Helen.

The poor oaf was called Roland. He was a lost boy of thirty-three who wandered about Europe playing a lute, which he carried on his back a la troubadour.

The slim young wife in the Western pants should have counted me a blessing. What if she had that poor oaf Roland cluttering up her nursery patio, twanging away on his lute.

Roland might have diverted the babies, but they seemed quite able to amuse themselves. They were always poking their fingers in each other's eyes, their own noses and mouths or worse. They were a little too fat for my taste but really remarkable when you thought that they had sprung from between those boy-slim loins.

At last the slim young wife in the Western pants had had all of me she could bear, a nerve beneath the left eye was beginning to twitch. She held the eye cupped in a thin, brown hand and began to blurt, "Brandon — your father — he's down by the pool." She whisked up the two adorable babies and fled away.

Brandon had not run to fat like Helen, he had gone to marshmallow. The old, flabby time had come. Lord knows, he had fought it off long enough. If they ever hung the British in effigy in Hollywood the dummy would look like Brandon in a bathing suit with a bowler hat on his head and a tightly furled umbrella in his hand.

Still, he had most of his hair. It was white unless he dyed, but he had it. The sagged face was still beautifully handsome. Oh, I understood them all — all the falling-down-before, swooning-away, running-after type ladies. I even understood the new, young wife in the Western pants. The last wife wishing she had been the first.

The first was named Edythe, the mother of the poor oaf.

She now ran a tearoom near Stratford. Funny what sticks in your mind — the only thing I knew about her was that she was Edythe and that she had a degree in literature from London University. I wondered if she ever recited sad sonnets as she served up the bath buns?

"Hello, Brandon," I said, "I'm going on the stage."

Brandon took off his dark glasses and stared agonized, into the sun.

"Why, for Christ's sake? It's a mug's game. When you're young it's all cake, when you're old nobody wants you. Nobody wants you when you're old." Two tears started out of his eyes and over his cheeks. He put the glasses back on.

Brandon was not entirely unwanted. Oh, he had had his bad times after the divorce. He was no longer the rage in Hollywood but he was not unwanted. He was Professor Pickles of TV fame.

His series went on while other's ratings fell and were dropped. Brandon may have been put out to pasture in his own mind but Palm Springs was clover compared to Central Park West.

Brandon had a whole new bank of life, what with reruns and residuals and co-production participations. Brandon had lucked out. Brandon had never been a very good actor. Beautiful and resonant, yes! Good, no! He had just pulled out all the stops and made that tone and the ladies had loved him.

Brandon lay there saying nothing. I thought perhaps he had gone to sleep. Brandon was perfectly capable of having a nice cry and waking up ready for twenty laps of the pool — having forgotten anything unpleasant that had gone before.

Brandon heaved a great Macready sigh and turned over to toast his backside.

"This is all Helen's idea, I suppose."

"No!" I said. "It's mine."

"Oh!" Brandon sat up instantly and began to function.

13

Only he was not really being Brandon, he was being "kindly old Professor Pickles." There was no problem of youth that Professor Pickles was not equipped to solve in half an hour.

Brandon's scriptwriters were well paid but even the best tend to lapse into clichés after so many weeks in a limited situation.

Brandon said that thousands of girls every year thought they wanted to become actresses but only one in a million had the "stuff" to stick it out, the discipline to train their minds and bodies, the self-discipline to give up pleasure for their art.

I had to be tested. How did I know I had talent? Brandon paused and cleared his throat.

"Just say," he went on, that I had inherited some talent from him, where was a young person to get training these days? In his day there was Rep and more Rep and the classics. Today there was only a lot of mumbling and intro-spection.

On the other hand, if I did have the "stuff" nothing would stop me no matter what the obstacle. It was, after all, up to me! A real actor did not have to ask how. A real actor found his way.

The speech was ended. Brandon plunged into the pool and began his twenty laps. Brandon might have nothing more to say to me but I knew he would have plenty to say to Helen.

It was only a fiction that they had had such a painful and bitter divorce that they had never spoken again. They talked to each other all the time. In the middle of the night they would take their telephones out into halls and shut doors. They would call each other and whisper behind hands cupped around receivers. They were like two teen-agers, who — Montague and Capulet — had to keep it a secret from the folks.

The bills went to their business managers instead of their

parents. Well, in a way, the business managers were their parents. They put them on allowances and saved for their future retirement the way parents saved for a college education.

When queried, Helen and Brandon said defensively that all those calls, Los Angeles to New York and New York to Los Angeles, were a business expense and therefore deductible.

Oh, they were sly and silly, thinking no one saw or heard. Perhaps Mr. Margolies and the slim young wife in the Western pants did not know. More likely they did not want to know, which is the same thing only much more positive.

That night, I could hear them as they whispered away, little hissing accusations of blame and guilt and fault and finally they ended up in giggles.

They were impossible and terrible and oh, so lovable. I loved them desperately. It was an impossible passion I had for them because for them I did not really exist. It was like standing behind a plate glass window and looking through at parents. Look but do not touch! They were in a museum with the other relics. The species had grown extinct.

As far as I was concerned, parents were something other people said they had while I had Brandon and Helen. And weren't they a useless pair? One look at them and it was bonjour insecurity. They couldn't take care of themselves let alone little things. Why they had ever reproduced themselves I don't know. I suppose at the time they were feeling warm and friendly and in some Olympian, Wagnerian way had to prove they were immortal and godlike.

Whatever they had said to each other about me on the telephone, Brandon said nothing more to me. Our visit went on as if there was nothing to discuss. We all sat out in the California sun trying to make enough conversation to last each day through.

Brandon and Helen had always been very naughty about

15

communicating. Not out of meanness, I'm sure, just careless and forgetful, their minds only upon themselves.

They had forgotten to tell me about the divorce. I had read about it in a newspaper.

When I asked Helen about it, she was astounded. Not about the item in the paper nor my learning about the divorce but about my being able to read. I was, after all, eight at the time. She called all her friends and Brandon too, I suppose, but she never discussed it with me until we were on the train coming back from Reno. By that time I had a fair idea that Brandon and Helen were not the sweethearts of Broadway any longer.

So I served out my time with Brandon in California and as I left Brandon gave me the standard goodbye. With much heavy breathing and many tears, he clutched me to his bosom and said, as he always did, "You may not believe I love you, but I do."

Now why would Brandon think I did not believe he loved me?

I T was all very fraught when I got back to New York.
Helen had on her acting face. Actors have two permanent
faces plus what biographers called their facets. There is the
face that is working and that is comedy; there is the face that
is not working and that is tragedy.

When Helen was not working, which was most of the
time, one had to pump up her knees and tell her she was
lovely and talented all the livelong day and Mr. Margolies
told her far into the night.

When Helen was working, it was very hard to get a word
in edgewise because Helen was always talking about her play,
her playwright, her designer, her company, her costumes, her
director, not to mention herself.

Rehearsals were about to begin for her summer tryout; the
apartment was full of her actors, her director, her costume
designer, not to mention her playwright.

When I came home her playwright had to be moved out
of my room into the maid's room. It was a very small maid's
room and the playwright, who had claustrophobia, broke out
and was constantly found rewriting in odd corners and eating
and drinking in all corners.

Helen said she wanted her playwright there, with her, so
she could read the rewrites as they came out of the type-
writer. In my opinion, the playwright wanted to be there

because he was too poor to stay in a hotel and it was still too cold to sleep in Central Park. That worn tweed jacket was not affectation, it was necessity.

Whatever the true truth, he was hungry, he drank and his sinus plagued him. I had found candy wrappers and a Benzedrine inhaler in my bureau drawer and an empty pint of rye in my closet down behind the shoe rack.

Mr. Margolies was in his element. He had all the theatrical housekeeping to do. He had to deal with the budget, the travel itineraries, the bus for the peasants, the limousine for Helen and himself. He had to check the swatches for Helen's costumes, the dimensions of the set, her hand props. Everything Helen was to touch, wear, sit on or look into became sacred, and Mr. Margolies was the keeper of the Priestess.

They had no time for me. No place for me, either, so I stayed in my room and looked out over the coming of the first leaves and the lovers in the park.

The hour of the French final marched steadily closer. The certainty of failure filled me with blessed relief. It was bliss to have no anxiety, to know my immediate future was marvelously predictable.

No wonder people who know exactly when they are going to die take it so well.

However, even in this state of euphoria, I noticed no one, not Brandon nor Helen, had said boo about what plans they might have made for my future.

The French final was a brilliant fiasco. I could not read the questions, which were in French, let alone answer them. I sat for a while listening to the scratching of pens on paper, the sighs, the nervous shifting in seats and then I boldly signed my name at the top of the blank page, left the classroom and took a dear little taxi down to corner Helen at Silver's.

Silver's is the great costumers, a gigantic attic for all who would play dress-up. I love looking at the feathers and the ropes of rhinestones, the velvet coats, the racks of crino-lines, the baskets of rich stuffs.

Helen's designer was building her things from scratch, the rest he would have to find out of open stock for summer stock.

Helen was being fitted for her third-act ball gown. She stood pinned up in muslin on their sheet-covered platform, a deep exclamation line between her brows and her mouth straight.

Helen usually liked fittings better than anything but losing five pounds. Today she was peevish. She had been kept waiting by some new preempting television people.

To Helen they were not spectacular, they were merely an unpleasant spectacle.

"Leslie, dear," she was saying to her designer, "the meas-urements I gave you were quite correct. My waist is just the same."

Leslie dear hissed venom in jets between the row of pins in his mouth and jabbed away at the muslin in infantile rage.

From beyond the curtained, partitioned walls of the fitting room came a voice resonant, pear-shaped, used to making its way to the second balcony. It said, "Have you seen Helen Shell? Must be fifty if she's a day." Helen twitched and was pricked by an agony of pins.

"Stand still, do!" hissed Leslie dear.

"Who is that?" Helen asked me.

"I don't know."

"Go and see." It was a command royal.

I went but there was no one there but a padded draper's dummy, some cigarette butts and the scent of a ripe French perfume.

"There was no one," I said to Helen. "There was no one there."

Helen was rigid in fury. Leslie almost in tears.

"I don't suppose you'd tell me if there were," said Helen bitterly.

"Unfair, Helen, falsely accused!"

"The young don't know what it is to grow old."

Poor Helen always got herself into that kind of illogical cul-de-sac but I knew what she meant. Until this year, I had always felt that people who were old or fat or ill had chosen to be so. I supposed they had some choice in the matter. As when their throats were creepy crepey or their upper arms hanging flabby, they sometime chose to wear satin and décolletage.

Then, suddenly this spring, I began to see as I looked in the mirror that time can go on without the will. That when it is your season to grow older you cannot exchange it for another year.

"Helen," I said, "what about this summer? What have you thought of doing with me?"

"Oh," Helen gave a heart-twisted wail. Her grief, her anguish was acute, "can't you see I have a pain?"

"Yes, Helen, I see."

I went away at once. Sometimes the reality of me was too much for Helen to have to deal with. As long as I could be popped in and out of schools and camps, Helen had had a difficult child, but then all children are difficult. Now, I was not poppable any longer. I was too large for the nest and beginning to be awkward for her.

I should have known better but I sent Brandon a wire.

"What plans have been made for my future?" I received a wire back from Pickles Productions, cable address Pickprod, "Mr. Brandon on location unable to locate."

Either the Pickprod organization was more vague and indifferent than I thought or Brandon was evading his responsibility.

He had done it before with the poor oaf Roland — why not me?

4

IN the end it was Mr. Margolies who arranged it all. I felt that I really ought to tell him how things stood at Miss Rose's. After all it had been he who had pulled some upper-class, untheatrical strings to have me admitted there in the first place.

I went round to the Ideal Rehearsal Studios where Helen's play was putting itself together. Rehearsal space in Manhattan is very hard to come by and one has to pay dear and take what one gets with grace and gratitude. Still, must it all be so dreary and flyblown? The Ideal was middle-of-the-road horrible — gangrene walls encrusted with finger marks, glazed over with dirt.

Rehearsals always look like a madhouse if you don't know what's going on. This one more so than ever. They would not be carrying a full company, just Helen, her daughter, and the man.

The rest of the cast, the maid, the friend of the daughter and the butler, would be picked up in each theatre where they were to play. Before Helen arrived that maid and friend and butler would rehearse without them and when Helen did arrive, they would all have a technical rehearsal, a dress rehearsal, and a run-through together before the opening.

Now, to fill in the gaps at the Ideal Studios, the director,

21

the playwright and the stage manager were reading the maid, the friend and the butler.

It looked like remedial therapy time at a badly run mental institution.

I liked watching rehearsals. I had a theory that if you could see someone else play a part you'd know better how to do it yourself. You can rehearse a play a thousand times and not know what you are doing wrong. But if you can see someone else walk through it, the right piece of business, the best cross becomes apparent in an instant.

I suppose there are people who learn best from experience but I think one learns best from example, the lesson in the flesh, the living rule.

Look at all the people who smash their lives again and again without having any new thoughts at all. Experience does not teach much but a tolerance of pain. One simply learns to endure dols and dols of agony.

When Brandon and Helen had been in their play in New York, I had gone to their rehearsal and later sometimes I was allowed to go to the theatre on matinee days — but only to see the third act.

If they were feeling grand and had nothing better to do, they let me stay till the evening performance. Nanny was sent out to fetch in supper and I was allowed to potter at the dressing tables and cozy with them on their resting cots and color quietly while they napped.

I never saw the first two acts but I saw the third. The third act was all fantasy and children are supposed to like fantasy.

Well, they don't. They like bread and butter, small beer and cheese — they like home truths and not too many rules to remember. All those dragons and fairies and transformations and disappearances scare the hell out of them.

They are just bearable for children who have loving parents, stationary home sites, regular baths and lots of warm, wooly towels. Even secure children have a nightmare now and again.

But my only home was that dressing room on lucky matinee days and so that third act that was supposed to be so beautiful and reassuring made me turn cold and sweat.

In that third act, Brandon and Helen, who were playing dead, found an abandoned ghost child and made up a family. It was wartime, remember, and everybody liked to think there was a life after death just like the life back home.

I did not think it was a beautiful third act. I had a terrible feeling that if Helen and Brandon were to die, they wouldn't take me along, they would leave me with Nanny.

I wanted to ask them what was going to happen to me in case of their sudden death, but by the time I had thought out the question, the play had closed and obviously they had not thought of me at all.

Actually it turned out not too badly for me. I had the business of childhood to attend to; school and camp and teeth and learning how to survive the tyrants and the bullies.

Passive resistance is best, the only way for the oppressed, the downtrodden and children. If you just sit on the railroad tracks, sodden and inert, you are very difficult if not impossible to deal with. After they have carried you to jail and you have fasted awhile, they have to let you go and give you modified self-government.

What a pity to learn how to survive just as childhood is over. All that useful knowledge gone to waste. When you grow up, no one ever treats you that badly ever again. I mean even the worst of grownups have recourse to law. While there is no place the young can even file a complaint.

I waited till there was a rehearsal break and followed Mr. Margolies out to the Coke machine. Mr. Margolies put in a dime and pulled out a Coke which he kindly offered me. I shook my head.

"Mr. Margolies, I've failed French and I'm going on the stage."

"Well, well," said Mr. Margolies. "Well, well, well." Mr. Margolies had a tendency to repeat himself.

Mr. Margolies found the perfect solution to both my problems. He arranged for me to go to the Old Barn as an apprentice for the whole summer season and since I had to report to the Old Barn before the end of the term at Miss Rose's, I was allowed to pass out of school as a non-graduating senior.

My last interview with Miss Rose, when I went like a furtive, scholastic mouse to pick up my locker crumbs, was very nearly pleasant.

"Now that you are going back to your own world," Miss Rose said all confidential and cozy, "we hope you won't forget what you have learned here."

It was as if I were a foreign exchange student, without standing, who had been allowed to audit a course or two, without credit. There had been no real necessity for me to learn the language and although I had been a burden, now that I was going, all my strange ways were to be forgiven with exquisite condescension.

Mr. Margolies was very pleased with himself at getting me into the Old Barn.

"There now," he said when he told me his news, "what do you think of that? You can't do better than the Old Barn. What do you say to that?"

I said, "Thank you, Mr. Margolies."

The Old Barn had the best reputation of any summer theatre in the country. They ran a ten-week season. Helen's play was to close the season so I could spend the summer rubbing my nose in greasepaint and then Helen could pick me up and bring me home.

The apprentices were to arrive two weeks early to open up the theatre.

I was free — supervised by the Old Barn, but free to make my way through the land of make-believe into the real world, where I would find my true love and he me and we would have a lovely baby to take care of as no one had taken care of me.

THE HUMAN COMEDY

5

I BECAME an apprentice, that is, one bound by agreement, to serve another for a certain time, in consideration of instruction in an art or trade and formerly usually of maintenance—*Webster's Collegiate Dictionary*.

There were seven apprentae. We had come to Eastport — one hour away from New York City by train — and a world away from any reality. We stood about the musty, dusty stage of the Old Barn awaiting our first instruction; each displaying his own affectation of maturity — a cigarette, an ankle bracelet, a weather-telling watch, a pair of false eyelashes — all too old for camp, too young for summer in Europe alone.

Three boys, four girls, Bennington, Sarah Lawrence, Barnard and me. Harvard, Yale and New Mexico. All except New Mexico had been Eastern-bred, nanny-reared and overgroomed.

One governor's daughter, one banker's daughter, one ambassador's daughter. One cloak-and-suiter's son, one investment broker's son and one rancher's son.

Although I was the youngest, I ranked them all because in this land of the blind I had two one-eyed theatrical parents.

Among us we had fifteen divorces, twenty-one stepbrothers and -sisters and four analysts. How any of us managed to function, I do not know.

None had come because of any personal merit. We were all examples of nepotism. We were legacy and bequests, all failures elsewhere in our own right.

We did not have to pay for our instruction but we were not maintained as formerly. We had to pay our own board and room and supply our own toothpaste and Scotch.

We were officially in service to the management of the Old Barn. But the owner of the Old Barn was the Stage Society who were in New York. Here they had a hired manager, a box office man, a stage manager, an assistant stage manager, and a scene designer.

We were, in fact, to be the slaves of the scene designer and expected to do his every bidding.

The stage manager was the overseer and he gave these facts to us as he had to others like us at the beginning of every summer for seasons past.

We were all to be domiciled at the home of Mrs. Fritchie; she put up the apprentices every year because she was a loyal supporter of the theatre. He did not add that she needed this summer money so she could go to Florida every winter.

"So now," the stage manager said, if we would all go along in the theatre station wagon that would haul us and the props and the furniture all through the summer, it would take us to Mrs. Fritchie's where we could settle in, change into our work clothes and be back in an hour to open up the playhouse for business.

We all began to group up for the first sitting in the station wagon, when the boy I had been watching and who had been watching me said, "Hello." He looked like the boy who stood on the burning deck, very proud and resolute but liable to be burned and sunk if he did not watch out. "Hello," he said, "I'm Simon Furtwangler."

"I'm Diana Bradon." Just that much of me seemed to cheer him up. He smiled a lovely dawn-is-really-breaking-after-a-long-dark-night smile.

"We're going to be buddy chum pals," he said.

"How can you tell?"

"Look at the rest of them. They are walking wounded, parlor neurotics. We are ruined forever — we were blighted at birth. Come on, I'll give you a ride in my new toy." I did not feel blighted but I believed Simon must be right.

His new toy was much nicer than an overstuffed station wagon. His new toy was a baby-blue Mercedes-Benz convertible.

"Look at that," said Simon, pointing to the canvas top. "It's made of human skin."

I shuddered.

"You don't seem impressed," Simon said reprovingly. "You can't beat that old Third Reich technology."

"Why did you buy it?" I asked, "or are you one of those 'don't let's be beastly to the Germans, don't let's be hostile to the Hun' types?"

"Buy it?" Simon was incredulous. "I didn't buy it — it was a bribe."

I laughed nervously.

"Laugh if you will," said Simon, "but in all my years in analysis, I've learned that everything is the guilt and the gelt." Simon said solemnly, "Sidney and Shirley are feeling very guilty. The toy is to try and buy off their guilt pangs."

"Why do they have guilt?"

"They have guilt because they are Germans who escaped Hitler and wish they were English who had stuck out the blitz. They have guilt because they have abandoned me, their first and only begotten son, and run off to play with their flesh and the devil."

"Why do they have gelt?" I was fascinated with my new pal.

"Because they are the S & S Modes, Sid and Shirl. You wouldn't believe how vulgar they are."

"The Modes?"

"And Sid and Shirl. Shirl is tanned like an old Cossack saddle. Comes from lying out on Florida beaches in the winter. She wears plastic transparent shoes and paints her toenails amputation red. She wears sequined peekaboo chiffon cocktail dresses. Get the picture?"

"I do," I said, "indeed I do."

"Sidney's got hair growing out of his shoulders and his stomach hangs over his shorts. But worst of all, Sid says things."

"For instance?"

"Sid says buying from Germans is just good business because they can pay more reparations to Israel."

"Oh, dear."

"They are too hideous to be let in anywhere. They think it's because they are immigrants when actually it's because they are horrors."

Lucky me to have Brandon and Helen. Perhaps they weren't loving but they weren't horrors. Or were they?

"Sid and Shirl are amazed that they could have produced anything out of their flesh that is not gross." Simon turned a profile. "Regard, I am pale and non-hirsute."

"You are beautiful," I said, and it was true.

"Have I told you about my IQ?"

"Please, no."

"It's alarmingly high, like a fever. The testers take one look at the tests and re-test to be sure they have not made a mistake. Sid and Shirl don't like to have me around the house, they find my great brain a strain. I've been bought into the best schools. Places they won't let Sid and Shirl be seen for fear they might frighten the other parents."

"You're the Harvard," I said.

"Oh yes," Simon nodded. "Sid says any son of his should be a gift to Harvard."

"Is that why you went?"

"Naturally. Before I left, Sidney called me into his office.

He was chewing on a cold cigar and playing patty-cake with
his fingertips. He said he felt we ought to have a talk. It
occurred to me he was going to tell me his version of sex. But
no, he wanted to talk to me about success. He said you
couldn't be too careful about success. He said he had heard
that up at Harvard they had a publication called the *Crimson* and he said that if I was going to succeed I ought to
begin by being the editor. Not to let them get away with
making me assistant editor or anything second-rate like that.
And I said, well, what about being President of the University, would that suit him and he said no, editor or nothing.
Then he asked me how I was fixed for cash and I said all
right and he gave me an enormous check and got on the
phone to the mills and I went away quietly."

"I'm sorry," I said.

"I don't mind about the check," said Simon. "They are
just trying to divert me."

"Divert you from what?"

"Life."

"What would divert you?"

"Maybe dying."

"Are you working on the *Crimson?*"

"I don't even read it."

"Does that divert you?" I smiled.

"It helps the guilt and the gelt complex."

Of course, I thought, how sensible. I thought Simon was
very grown-up, very philosophical. He was my buddy chum
pal all right.

"Are you going on the stage?" I asked Simon.

"Never."

"What are you going to do?"

"I don't know yet." His face clouded over. "I'm looking for
work. I believe if I find work to do I'll find my identity. Are
you going on the stage?" he asked me.

"Oh, yes."

"Why?"

I told him about Brandon and Helen and the boys and the babies and about the poor oaf Roland. I told him I thought I ought to do something till I found my true love.

"Yes," Simon said sadly when I had finished, "the stage is much the best for you."

6

GOING away to be an apprentice in summer stock was like going to sea. We were brought on board two weeks early to get our sea legs and to make everything shipshape for the passengers.

The Old Barn was a luxury cruise ship. Each play was a different port of call. The subscription patrons got the entire voyage, ten ports in ten weeks. But anyone could join the ship in any port as long as they had the price and we had the space.

Each opening night was a gala, each closing night a farewell ball. There was a restaurant and bar attached to the theatre that served dinner before the play and supper after the curtain, or if you liked you could sit and drink to the music of a tiny piano. The paper lanterns, the flying flags, the painted canopy only made the ship look more festive and contained as she drifted there upon the New England sea.

The local blue laws forbade performances on the Sabbath. On Saturday we painted. On Saturday night after the last noon we had a technical rehearsal — on Sunday night a dress rehearsal — on Monday afternoon a run-through and on Monday night we opened.

Then on Tuesday morning, the crew, for that is what we were called, began to build the new set for next week's play. On Wednesday afternoon, during the matinee, we hunted for props and furniture and set out the handbills for the coming week. On Thursday we built, on Friday we painted, on Saturday we painted. On Saturday night after the last performance we struck the old set and laid the groundwork for the new.

At two or three in the morning, we would go back to Mrs. Fritchie's for a rest and a shower and then come back to start our Sabbath all over again. The sea was our new religion.

Sunday afternoon the technical; the light, the scenery, the props, the curtain going up and down. Not much rest for the crew — up and down we went on an ocean of fun and work.

In the old days at the Barn, there had been a resident company who had lived there all summer, and had played all the parts in all the plays. Now there was a star system.

Each star came with his or her own package. Sometimes there were small parts and actors jobbed in to join the ship for that one week but for the most part we had the complete package.

The star came to us like cargo marked fragile or this side up. The advance man, that household equerry for the star, would come ahead and give us the royal commands. We drudges were driven to carry them out.

The scene designer, whose slaves we were, was just getting over a nervous breakdown, a sort of Captain Queeg in reverse. He was sure that we were out to wreck his sets, unfocus his lights, insert the wrong gelatins, break and befoul the borrowed furniture, lose the hand props and generally destroy his career.

He had been in display at Lord and Taylor too long while trying to pass his union tests. His mercantile years had done him great damage. The jolly show-must-go-on-it-will-be-all-right-on-the-night camaraderie had been purged out of him in his buy-cheap, sell-dear years.

We never actually plotted mutiny but we saw that if we

were not to go as mad as he under the strain of life at sea, we must divert ourselves.

Simon, who had been in analysis the longest, became our recreational and mental health director. Like little tots of rum and lime juice to ward off scurvy, Simon tacked notices for us on the call board:

> Subject, The Topic of the Day
> All Franz of Liszt
> Meet at Midnight
> Signed: S. FURTWANGLER

While we built and hung and sawed and painted and lifted, our conversations were full of Lynne and Alfred and Oscar and Josh and Gadge and Marlon.

> Attention! Symposium Tonight
> Kim Hunter, Kim Novak, Kim Stanley —
> the relative merits of —
> Signed: S. FURTWANGLER

> All Nouns of Association Come to Order
> An Ennui of Anouilh
> A Bertolt of Brechts
> A Thomas à Beckets
> A Duchess of Albees
> A Merde of Genets
> Bring your own beer!
> Signed: S. FURTWANGLER

The scene designer forbade any further postings on the call board. The next day across the back of a flat, in great red letters was written:

> A Call to the Catacombs —
> Bring Your Own Lions

When we had a spare moment and thought we might not be discovered, we sat in dark corners of the house and watched them at work. The stars and their supporters, athletic and otherwise. The playwrights and the directors, the old trying to be young, the mediocre trying to shine like stars, the endless talk, the fights, the slights, the pecking order of sex.

And in the catacombs of Mrs. Fritchie's attic, where we had gone underground, we talked acting, the method, sense memory, the motor, the comedy reading, the build, the pause and Stanislavsky!

It all seemed like a lot of fuss and talk over nothing to me. One either had the talent for the work or one didn't, and if one had the talent one either had the opportunity to do the work or one didn't.

The great single flaw of actors was that they couldn't keep themselves still. They wriggled and grimaced and sawed the air; they tore passion to a tatter. The audience hadn't a hope of seeing them for all the commotion they caused.

When I had a part to play, I was going to sit still as a cat. I was going to sit and stare until the audience got tired of watching all that waste motion and looked at me.

Having decided this was the way of truth I began to practice being still and doing absolutely nothing. It became my thespic discipline.

Of course, I knew that sooner or later I would have to say some lines so I hummed a bit to enlarge my resonance cavities and I breathed a lot in and out.

Simon was my buddy chum pal. As for the rest of the crew, the voyage grew longer and they were a boring lot. We had bumped against each other too often and had disbanded into splinter groups. Simon and I became a group of two. I moved out of Bennington's room and into Simon's. I wasn't invited to move, it just happened that it was more convenient for the cause.

We now had a master project that was consuming all our after-hours fun time. We had begun a campaign to get the local movie house to show a festival of old Vera Hruba

Ralston films. It had been Simon's idea, not mine, but I helped.

We were behaving in this hostile fashion because one Friday we had sneaked off to the local cinema, where the manager had become surly and churlish about our taking in a bottle of crème de cacao and two straws. There was une crise and we were not admitted.

Simon decided to bend his great brain to total revenge.

He began the Vera Hruba Ralston campaign. The telephone calls, the releases to the papers, the letters from religious groups, school children, shut-ins. No progress so far but persistence is everything, Simon says.

I addressed envelopes and signed phony names, made phone calls. I liked living in Simon's room.

We sat warm and sung on Simon's bed. He, writing a plea from the Veterans of Foreign Wars, I practicing my breathing when suddenly I thought about the time when all this would be over and it was panic in the chest.

I threw myself on Simon.

"Can we go on being buddy chum pals when the summer is over?"

"Yes."

"Can we go on being buddy chum pals forever?"

"Yes."

"Oh, Simon," I said, "I've gotten a taste of being unlonely and I don't think I could go back to the other."

I was so overcome I turned out the light and attacked Simon physically in the flesh. I suppose I thought nothing would do for me but giving myself to him in total physical surrender. I was not ladylike, I should have waited until I was asked.

It was a little awkward but it was the only way I knew of keeping him from slipping away like Brandon and Helen to places where I could not follow and was not wanted.

"Oh, dear," I said, when I turned the light back on, "I've

had my way with you but I think I have been forward and demanding."

"Not to worry," Simon said. "I should have gotten around to making love to you sooner or later except . . ." He paused.

"Except what?" I asked in fear he would tell me I was too ugly and gauche to want to pursue.

"Except I don't really think the flesh is of that much value."

"Why?" I said. "I love my flesh and yours."

"I've been conditioned by Sidney and Shirley, I suppose. They are at it all the time and it hasn't improved them noticeably."

"Lots of people believe in it and they turn out quite well."

"Oh," said Simon, "but that's the difference. They believe. Sid and Shirl don't believe in anything. One shouldn't commit adultery unless one believes in it."

"I don't think this is adultery," I said. "I believe this is fornication."

"Whatever it is," Simon said, "I can't make any real commitments until I find my life's work. Only the work lasts, that's my philosophy. Either espouse or eschew it."

"I want to espouse you, Simon. I do, I do." Simon shook his head reprovingly.

"Just read the obituary columns. They are all the same. Only the work is worth one of the better obituaries. Read them for yourself. Never 'Were you happy?' 'Did you love your wife?' Never 'Did your son make you proud of him?' Just the work. I want to have a really fine obituary, at least a full column in the *New York Times*, and maybe a picture. Yes, I want the picture, too."

"What if you don't find that sort of work?" I asked. "What if you just have to live out your life like everybody else?"

"Then," Simon said, "I will have a problem."

40

Obviously making love wasn't something that would make Simon want to live with me forever and ever. I felt badly about that. I wanted him to want me most. I felt negative. I felt like an enormous zero. I did not care what my obituary was going to be. I felt dead and unburied now.

"Do you want me to move back in with Bennington?" I whimpered.

"Good Lord, no."

I stayed of course because I wanted to, but my image of myself as a total love object had to be retouched considerably.

7

THE weeks sailed past; the plays were new, old, ancient. The players were the same. Quite suddenly the posters read, "Next week Helen Shell in *A Little Sacrifice*." The summer was almost over.

There had been portents and alarms. The first cool evenings had come bringing ladies in beaded sweaters and fur stoles. The Coke sales at the intermission had fallen off. Not many stayed to drink round the little piano on the terrace. I had ignored all the auguries but it was nearly closing time all the same.

And then I got the part.

Simon said it was Helen's guilt for having me alone all summer with only a hasty postcard now and again that caused her to allow me to play the daughter's friend.

But it was the gelt too, because even if I had to join a union and be paid a minimum wage, it might bring money into the box office to exhibit Helen Shell with a grown daughter.

The other apprentae muttered darkly that I had been privileged the whole summer long.

Could they not see that if it had been the other way around, if I had been apprenticed to their family businesses, I would have remained forever in the mail room while they would have been groomed to sit in vice president's chairs?

It was not such a grand inheritance. Five sides, five half-sheets of paper was all my part. I would have to be very still if I hoped to attract any attention with that.

The stage manager said I could do it. The assistant stage manager said I could do it. The assistant stage manager had rehearsed the apprentices in a one-act play and I had not disgraced myself.

My scene, my five little half-pages were to be played with Helen. Her character, the mother, has realized that the man is not a suitable husband for her daughter and she has decided to marry him herself to save her daughter from a fate worse than death, which in this play was the fate of being disillusioned with love.

In our scene she asked me if I thought her daughter would ever forgive her for what she was going to do and I said not until her daughter is grown-up and has a daughter of her own.

Helen saw that she would spend the years ahead alone and without love but said, as every mother knows, even the sacrifice of losing a child was a very little sacrifice if it would bring her child happiness.

The playwright must have been drunk, inhaling Benzedrine, and eating candy bars all at the same time when he wrote our scene.

I was rehearsed by the assistant stage manager according to the gospel brought by Helen's advance man. The maid and the butler were also put through their positions.

For some reason I never understood, Bennington was chosen to play the maid and New Mexico the butler. Bennington looked too sex-mad and New Mexico too homosexual to let into an otherwise already overwrought household.

The assistant stage manager read all the other parts. He was the mother, the daughter and the man. I kept seeing Helen's face pasted on his body, a sort of cartoon — his voice coming out of Helen's mouth.

I had paid that assistant stage manager no mind all summer. He was just good old Ernie. Suddenly he was the most important person in my life.

That's one of the tricky bits in the theatre. I suppose it's why most marriages don't last. A person one is working with can become the emotional center and everyone else is an outsider.

It hurts when you're the odd man out. I remember when Helen and Brandon were on tour with the war play. Brandon came offstage with his arm around his stage child. I was standing in the wings watching and I ran toward Brandon thinking he would take me in too. Brandon and his stage child just stood there staring at me. Finally the stage child said, "Who's that?" and Brandon said, "I don't know."

It's part of the magic in the transference of self. It's a little dangerous and terribly exciting. These are the thrills and the rides. After a while one acquires a taste for them and nothing else will do.

Simon was jealous of the assistant stage manager. Simon and Yale and Sarah Lawrence and Barnard sat like malevolent geese in the house, and hissed sighs of envy at us on the stage.

The scene designer came after them, an Egyptian after the Israelites, and drove them off with a scourge to build flats without straw. The scene designer was growing into a final stage of maniacal frenzy. Simon said that he had seen a little fleck of foam on the scene designer's lips.

The last notice of the season went up on the call board:

> Crew Report to Eastport General Hospital for
> Rabies Shots
> (Unsigned)

The designer cried, sobbing away on the paint rack. We were all silent and ashamed.

The frost between Simon and me melted with the Sabbath

and the technical rehearsal. Simon sat out front. He was to be my judge. I could trust no other.

The assistant stage manager had said I was all right. His actual words were, "You're better than I thought you would be," but only Simon could tell me truly.

There is not a soul in the theatre who can do the acting without that someone. It can be an agent, a director, a friend of the heart or the bosom, a wife, a husband, it can be your mother, but that someone has to be there to tell you what you're really doing.

You're out there flying and the someone is in the tower watching your progress, talking you onto the field.

It wasn't going to be my mother. Helen was not going to see me for her stardust. So my someone had to be Simon.

Helen came into the theatre early Sunday morning. She stood out in the house looking up at the lights, checking the sight lines, thinking of her play, her critics and her desire to work for the Stage Society in New York. And after a good, long look, Helen went down to place her hallmarks in her dressing room.

I had crew that morning. Helen passed me by a dozen times. Whenever she was in danger of having to focus on me, she put down her dark glasses from the top of her head, like a knight lowering his visor before the joust.

I was ready to try my lance against hers, to tilt before my peers, to be, if worst came to worst, unhorsed, but I did not lie to myself and I knew my hand shook, my heart beat, and my mouth was dry. There is no place more exposed and no place one can be so alone as a summer theatre on Sunday morning.

Mr. Margolies had brought Helen in her limousine. He passed me by as I was standing on a ladder hanging drapes. He looked up with awe.

"I hear you're wonderful, just wonderful." Mr. Margolies

looked terribly pleased. He was a proud stage father, he had a wife and a stepchild under his management.

I wish I had thought I was wonderful.

Saturday night after the strike, Simon and I had lain in bed, tired and exhausted. My head was on his chest. I heard his heart and my head moved up and down ever so gently as he breathed. We were still, silent, sensitive as only two listening people in a double bed can be.

"Tell me." My voice was very small and tight. Simon was so long a time answering I thought I had not said it aloud but only to myself. Simon lay staring up at the ceiling. I felt his eyes above me looking up. I heard him swallow, his chest stopped like a French lift with a sudden jerk and then began again.

"Everything's fine," Simon said. "Everything you're doing is fine."

"Tell me," I said more harshly.

"You're OK, really you are."

I turned over — away from his warmth.

"You are," he said.

"You lie," I said.

"No." Simon said it slowly and I knew he was going to tell me now. I braced myself for the news. It's always possible that one has no talent, that one's just a cold pudding called mediocre; which, as anyone knows, is the worst kind of pudding there is. One can face total failure or absolute brilliance but what one cannot face being is lukewarm dishwater — too good to throw out, too tepid to do any good.

"Go on, Simon."

"I wasn't lying," said Simon. "Everything you're doing is fine but —" He paused; I thought I would have an attack of vertigo and fall through time and space deaf with disaster before I heard what he was going to say. "It's not together," Simon said. "It's not one piece. The voice is fine, the hands, the face, the feet, the eyes; you move well — but it's all fragments, there's nobody there, no real character."

Two great hot tears started down the cheeks, I was lying on my side. One went over my nose and plopped into a nostril. I snuffled and the tear got sucked up into a sinus cavity. I began to cry in earnest. It really was unfair — to have decided to emigrate to Elysium and now they would not grant me a visa because I had no talent. I could not go back where I had come from. I was totally displaced. I would have to go to one of those camps and stand about, yellow and thin, behind barbed wire.

"What's the matter with you?" Simon demanded.

"I'm not any good," I sobbed. The desert of my desolation swept out from me to the rim of the sky.

"Jesus Christ," said Simon, "did you think you were going to spring fully clad from your own brow? Did you not plan to work at it?"

I wailed; friendless and naked in the frozen north.

"I didn't know," said Simon, "that you were going to be an amateur. I thought you were going to be a professional. I thought that you intended to perform a work of art, not accident."

I sat up and hit him as hard as I could. With one swift kick, he shoved me out of the bed. He turned on the light and looked down upon me.

"Well there you are," Simon said. "Down and out."

We began to laugh and laugh. By the time Mrs. Fritchie came up to see what all the commotion was, we had gotten our robes on and had begun to work on the scene.

"We're just rehearsing," we said.

"Oh," said Mrs. Fritchie, "I didn't mean to disturb you."

So by the technical rehearsal I was wary, scary, over-rehearsed, sick at my stomach, but ready. There does come a time even for cowards when you've got to try just to see what will happen.

47

No costumes, no makeup, no magic for a technical, just a very dry run to see if you can do the work. The long wait till they came to my scene in the third act. Simon's face out front as luminous as the face of a watch.

Simon said it was much better.

Helen said she was proud of her baby. Mr. Margolies hugged me without saying a word and for the first time, I hugged him back.

I myself thought it had not gone too badly, because the apprentae who had been green, grudging and hostile were full of a new respect.

I enjoyed the dress rehearsal, I began to see. I tried to explain that to Simon but I don't know if he really understood. When you're rehearsing, it's not that you don't see the other actors, the props, the set, the furniture — you do — but your vision is imperfect shapes, blurs, faded colors.

When you begin to play for the first time — begin to play your lines against the other actors' lines — you begin to see. For me it happened at the first dress rehearsal — sitting there on the set waiting for the curtain to go up, the lights getting warmer and warmer, then standing in the wings waiting for my entrance. Suddenly, like the first day of creation, I saw a face, eyes, wrinkles. I perceived a pattern in the carpet. I refocused my being and passed over into the magic circle.

At that dress rehearsal, I saw Helen, not Helen herself but the part she was playing. We had a moment apart from any other time or place. We existed and so did our acting selves.

If I had the skill, the magic, the fakir's stone, I could go away from that time and place and lead my ordinary life and then I could come back to that place and that time to that incredible instant I had created. I would be an actor.

I could not wait for the Monday run-through to see if it would happen again.

It did. I had made a new life. I could be another person

whenever I wanted to be. In the warmth and circle of the lights, there was the garden of enchantment, the wood of wonder, a place to appear and vanish and reappear.

All Simon had to say after the dress rehearsal was that the pieces had come together.

8

A<small>ND</small> then came the opening night. I was afraid it might be an anticlimax after the revelations of the past two days.

Oh, the mindless bliss of being stone dumb. I had forgotten about the audience. I had been so preoccupied with my powers, I had forgotten they had theirs. They are the "they" one hears of. The formless, faceless "they" without whom there is no element of chance in the void. They are kismet. No creation is free from it, not the creation of the universe, not the creation of man.

If one plays at creation, one plays at being God and no man, and perhaps not God can control the final judgment. Once it is started, once the curtain has gone up, there is no turning back from the judgment of fate.

One audience is not another; one performance is not another. Each time the curtain is raised, it begins again like the first day. One must wait until the curtain falls before you can know the final outcome.

They can be coaxed, cajoled, made to laugh, made to cry, to gasp, to shudder, to sit still as eternal night beyond the rim of lights. They can be made to applaud exits and entrances; they can be made to cough and rustle, but they cannot be made to give a favorable judgment. They alone will make the decision.

I remembered that opening night, remembered with a

blood fear, how I had seen players try to crook that judgment to themselves; and how I had seen them destroyed.

They decided to like me that opening night. What jubilation, what exultation and hosannas to the great faceless eye that had winked at me; a feasting, a drinking, a toasting to survival from the claw of the great black beast.

I was patted, caressed by the applause, knowing it might have gone the other way and that the razor claw might have been unsheathed with switchblade quickness.

Helen had come out kindly treated. The acting company was all alive — only the daughter had been bloodied. There had been a hiss and whisper from the pit that she had not pleased. They would have liked to see me in that part.

It was not I that had drawn her blood but she blamed me for it. I was an adversary she could see and touch, a foe she could accept and hope to defeat.

I had dressed behind an onstage flat with the maid and the butler, a little makeshift dressing room that befitted my station.

The daughter had a dressing room of her own, a cell of loneliness in which to weep unnoticed as she removed her makeup and faced into the mirror on the wall that told her the long summer had been for nothing.

Helen was receiving in her bower of flowers. That audience was an old friend of hers. They came to speak her fair. With them came those outriders of the city, those couriers who must be first back to the marketplace with the news. They vied with each other in their eagerness to go back down that road to the city waving palms and singing psalms of praise for Helen.

Two or three even found their way to me behind the onstage flat and prophesied they would praise me also in the city.

The husband of the play forgot the tortures Helen had put

him to for the last ten terrible weeks. He foolishly spoke to
her of "their" triumph. His end, poor thing, was near.

Mr. Margolies was arm in arm with the president of the
Stage Society. They were surrounded by a ring of men in soft
black hats who dealt in bricks and mortar, percentages, ice,
and weekly grosses.

The theatre party ladies came backstage to get a firsthand
look at Helen. They were like a swarm of Mongol horse
traders in their caracul coats. They all but pried open her
mouth and counted her teeth.

Helen suffered herself to be poked and prodded and
sniffed because if the Mongols found her suitable they could
guarantee enough ticket sales to fill the arena. The ladies
bought Helen. So did the Stage Society. The word was, bring
the package in.

The libations of thanksgiving were to be poured at the
country estate of the president of the Stage Society. I was
allowed to ride in the limousine with Helen and Mr. Margolies. I was being escorted by the Queen Mother into the
court circle, to be presented to my peers.

I would not go without Simon. He was not permitted to
ride in the limousine. He tagged along in the toy. I had seen
Helen's face when she understood I did not intend to go
without him. I had seen her face again when she saw the size
and price of his Mercedes charger. Here was no country-poor
knight.

Helen kept me by her side. We were welded arm in arm. I
was the fairy-tale princess who had, for my own safety, been
entrusted into the keeping of the kindly woodcutter, the
gamekeeper, the three good fairies. Now the evil spell of
youth was believed to be over and I had been returned to my
rightful place.

Helen had never played the injured Queen in *The
Winter's Tale* but she was Hermione to the navel.

I was presented, made over, approved, admired and
treated with all courtesy. There were a goodly number of

possible suitors. Helen named each and then discussed them, Nerissa to my Portia. She would have none of them for me, and I would have none of them for myself. Only Simon would do.

Helen decided to grant Simon, the strange prince of the East, an interview, a personal dismissal.

Simon was a match for Helen and then some. He killed her with undergraduate kindness, he cut her to the ground with the deference youth owes age, he blinded her with a glimpse of the gold in his jewel-encrusted coffers. Helen gave o'er.

I was allowed to leave the ball with the prince of the East, but not until Helen had reminded him that I was after all a child, too young for the marriage contract and too simple to know my own mind.

We left the summer palace and went out for a hamburger with the apprentae. We were all bound together that night by a sudden rush of affection. As at the end of any school term, there was a frantic address-taking and promising to meet again.

I didn't care if I never saw any of them again as long as I lived if only I could see Simon always. The ship was putting into port, the cruise was almost over. If we could not make the change from sea to land, we would be les petites enfants perdus. I had remembered some of Miss Rose's French after all.

I also remembered the word "Fin" at the end of the movie. The whole week was a week of "fin." On Wednesday, I was eighteen and got to make my last wish before officially leaving childhood forever.

I wished to be driven down to New York by Simon in the toy. I did not wish to be taken home by my mother.

The birthday party was held after the Wednesday night performance. The piano played "Happy Birthday," there was cake, courtesy of the management. Just as I blew out the candles, my eyes looked over the eighteen little flames into

Helen's face. I saw she wished my great age were not public knowledge.

I blew with all my might; the flames vanished, the piano played on and on.

Simon bought a bottle of champagne to toast me when we were alone at Mrs. Fritchie's. Simon said being eighteen was so tribal a ritual that the champagne was obligatory.

I drank most of it and giggled myself to tears. The idea of leaving our dear little room was agony. It made the tears run. I played the whole scene with acres of musical-comedy dialogue about holding back the ship and time, about keeping us forever safe here in our warm feathered nest. I made appalling crude love to Simon who humored me and held me close as I sobbed bitter mascara-riddled tears into his armpit.

"I will have you for my own true love. I will I will."

"There, there," said Simon patting me on the back like a young father walking the room with a colicky baby. "There, there."

I slept away all my old chorus-girl platitudes and awoke without a headache. But all the lead was still in the heart. The terrible knowledge of nothing enduring under the sun dragged me down to the finality of the closing night.

I refused to pack my bags. I put everything in pillow slips, wadding clothes in like a sailor's portable gear. It seemed less inevitable, less like walking the plank if I carried no baggage.

The only bright sight was the theatre marquee of the Eastport movie. It read:

THIS WEEK

BY POPULAR DEMAND

VERA HRUBA RALSTON FESTIVAL

We drove around and around the block, honking the horn; then dizzy with triumph and achievement, Simon headed for the turnpike and the wicked city. As Simon said:

"One's good works live after one."

9

WE made the change from sea to land but we lost something in the translation. I think it was the illusion of being outside the reach of the fates that did us in. We had not truly been our own masters, nor steered the ship. We had only presumed we set the course and you know how angry presumption makes the gods.

Once again in the city we were undeniably in the hands of the Moerae and they flung us along to our destiny. We had driven very fast down the turnpike fleeing from the poppies of memory. We ran to the canopied entrance of the apartment on Central Park West. As we stopped, Simon gave a cry.

"What is it?" I asked him.

"I'm having total recall pangs," he said. "I used to live here."

"No."

"Yes."

"When?"

"I was quite small, five or six. I remember being taken to the park by a colored girl in a white dress and white nurse's shoes. How she loved those nurse's shoes. She thought they gave her professional status."

"What was her name?"

"I don't know."

"Not total recall."

"Small block."

"Did you like her?"

"Yes," Simon smiled slowly, "yes, I did. She was Catholic and sometimes she took me to church and let me light candles."

"How lovely."

"I can smell those candles now," said Simon, "and by the way, her name was Sheila."

"Oh, Simon, what happened to Sheila?"

"I don't know," said Simon. "We moved to Park Avenue and Sheila was replaced by a French mamzell."

"With French status?"

"Lots of French status," Simon said, "and a lot of filthy postcards." He shook his head. "Sid and Shirl thought they were being so grand on Park Avenue with a French whore to walk me to the park. Ah, well . . ." Simon looked up at the apartment house. "That's all the recall for today. Do you want me to come in with you?"

"No," I said quickly, "we start rehearsal tomorrow and I've got to sort out all these pillow slips."

"All right," Simon said, "see ya."

"Sure," I said, "see ya." I ran, leaving the pillowcases for the doorman to lug inside.

Rehearsal for the Stage Society was quite different from rehearsal for a summer package. What had seemed a good thing in summer stock would clearly not do for Broadway.

The daughter was fired and replaced with a hard-faced ingenue well-known about the town; the old retainers were to be played by a character couple who always played old family retainers; the husband was replaced by a movie name who had never acted in New York but who was supposed to sell tickets in case Helen did not, and I was to stay in the hope they could make a few mother-daughter press releases out of me.

The rehearsals were held in the Stage Society's town house. It had once been an embassy and had an air of international decadence. We had the privilege of using the chilly ballroom, a cold, leaden echo of a room, with a parquet floor and clouded mirrors. No coffee cartons here, no Coke machine, all was sotto voce, Venetian court intrigue.

There was a new pecking order and very little feed for me; no one to talk to me. If this was the real theatre, it wasn't much fun. It was cold cream of wheat after the summer fare.

Helen certainly did not want to talk to me. Her director had gone out of her corner into the Stage Society's and rarely spoke at all. The hard-faced daughter spoke only to people with influence and clearly I was not one. The maid and the butler spoke when spoken to. They did not speak to me for fear of reprimand but they were willing to speak, which was strangely comforting. They nodded and smiled when no one was looking. They made me feel a child again in that time when my only friend was Nanny and she had been allowed no familiarity.

The Hollywood star never learned his lines, never took off his vicuña overcoat, and talked all the time. He told endless stories of his life in films. It was rather like being shut up in a rococo icebox with an old movie magazine.

Helen did not rant or rave as I would have expected. Helen was a new Helen to me, grim, tense, nerves coiled tensile tight. I had the feeling that if she let go, she would carom off those brocaded walls out of any redeemable control.

Even Mr. Margolies did not speak to me. He was now low man on the tribal pole. He was here to defer, conciliate, and try to press rehearsals in spite of the Hollywood star's endless chatter and failing memory for the present work.

I was certainly able to sit as still as I liked and nobody noticed me.

We drove from the apartment to the Stage Society in a hired limousine, full of anticipated dread. We drove home again in the silence of realized doom.

If I had been wiser in the ways of the theatre, I would have known at once that we were destined to failure. I was in a flop and everyone knew it but me. They knew it in their bones and in their livers and lights. They did not say it, no hellfire hot enough for the one who said it first.

Failure was a ritual of the playhouse into which I had not been initiated. I was a novice. There was no remembered agony to chill my blood. My heart still tweeted like a piccolo playing a Sousa march. All the stones of their oncoming despair could not weigh me down.

It was no wonder they did not talk to me. How can you explain failure to a child? Besides, there is always the hope that they may be wrong. Everyone had seen the miracle of miracles happen, had seen a sure flop become a hit. Well, perhaps not seen it themselves but heard of it, had at least been told the legend of *Abie's Irish Rose.*

But just in case their feelings were right and this play was the dog of the season, they began looking about for someone to blame. Blame would have to be placed in someone's hand. Blame is a game of button, button, who has the button. No one wants it to rest on him.

The Hollywood star was the early favorite, the logical candidate. Clearly, if he did not say his lines, there was no hope of putting on the play. And say them he would not. He would not let the script out of his hands. He would not put on his glasses to read the words, he would not say them from memory. He had tried to learn them and could not. Each time his cue was given and it was his turn to speak it reminded him of a story of his early days in films and he was off.

Any word that had been uttered twenty years ago by C. B. De Mille was evergreen in his memory. Every syllable was repeated with gestures while Helen, the daughter and the retainers stood and waited and pretended to listen.

The director sat head in hands. I suppose at his prayers. The playwright went to the men's room to vomit and drink and inhale and the Hollywood star talked on and on until it was time to go to lunch or to fittings or home. He would go anywhere but on with the play.

Simon hung about in a hotel lobby down the street, waiting for me to have a break. You wouldn't think I'd be needed very much, not with my little bit to say, but since it was one of the few scenes the director could rehearse without the Hollywood star, we rehearsed it often to fill in the gap.

Simon and I became diminished by the clock to a kind of now-or-never gaiety. It was like having booked ahead and paid for New Year's Eve and then being obliged to enjoy it. Simon decided that what was needed was deferment. He said that when we played Boston, he would show me Harvard and surely then in Cambridge, across the River Charles, we could be ourselves again.

Simon packed up and went to school. We packed and went on the road: Wilmington, Philadelphia, Washington, New Haven, Boston.

Helen loved to tour. I had not known that. I had only heard the complaints, the difficulties, the inconveniences, the cries of fatigue. Helen loved motion, escape and perpetual flight.

Now that the production was on the stage, the Hollywood star must, willy-nilly, answer Helen with something other than ancient reminiscences. Helen was at center stage. The lights focused on her and she grew young on the feast of fish.

On tour Helen got lots and lots of fish. All actors work for fish. You see them like greedy seals on sunny rocks at feeding time lined up for the curtain call, waiting for fish. Praise, approbation, favor, honor, applause, buckets full of lovely fish, that's what actors work for.

On tour there are extra helpings of newspaper interviews, late-night radio people, early morning TV people, ladies' club tea people; awards, plaques, medals, statuettes; baskets full of fish.

I got a taste of fish myself and was utterly spoiled for a lifetime of ordinary compliments. Newspapers photographed us for the entertainment page, and captioned us Queen and Princess of Thespis, "daughter-in-waiting," "family tradition observed."

Helen acted the mother on and off stage. Interviewed by gossips of public communication channels, Helen said, "Of course I'm not jealous of Diana's youth. We all have an obligation to our young. They are our future." Or my favorite, "The gap between the generations is closed by the bridge of truth."

Helen was just full of little nuggets of wisdom.

The play was on the Stage Society Subscription and did a bit of business on its own. The reviewers were kind. Kind to Helen, kind to playwright, kind to daughter and retainers; a mention to me and even kind to the Hollywood star, which we all felt was unfair since although he now spoke lines, they were the words of his own choosing. Helen never knew what he was going to say. Once in Philadelphia he had talked a lot of gibberish and when he stopped, Helen stood stunned trying to sort something out she could use for a cue. Then he turned his back to the audience, smiled and whispered to Helen, "You go on, dear."

We should have been grateful, I suppose, that they did not run him off the stage and out of town, which was what we thought he deserved.

He too was interviewed and photographed. He covered Helen with diamonds of praise for all her help in this, his new medium. He wrapped her in sables for her patience with an old beginner. He took me by the hand at the curtain call and pushed me out front for bows with him. He said we were two newcomers, though there was a difference in our ages and he made a wry and funny face.

He loved to make these little curtain speeches. He told stories of the company's dismay when they sat round to hear him read at the first rehearsal. He told stories of us as our better selves. He was charming. Helen was charming. Everyone was full of charm all listening to the lullaby of the local sirens of the press. Oh, if only we had stayed in those waters, if only we had drifted ashore on those friendly strands.

By the time we put into Boston harbor, all thought of failure had gone out of their heads.

I dashed out to meet Simon in Cambridge; only eight minutes from Park Street.

10

THAT day began the era of the green book bag. Simon had it slung over his shoulder. He said it was a must, otherwise one might not be recognized as an undergraduate. It made me laugh to see such sport because Simon could not have been anything else.

We saw the Coop, we saw the Brattle Street ladies in jazzy new settings. We saw Widener Library, Simon's home away from home, and we saw the Yard and then we went over to Cardullo's and filled the green book bag full of goodies and took them around to Simon's digs.

Simon was able to live off the campus because his analyst said he could. Simon's digs were on a dingy street behind Memorial Hall. His landlady's name was Mrs. Mulcahy, a myopic Irish saint of venality.

Simon had taken her artist's suite, as she called it; it was her attic, two big rooms and a bath, the parlor and the kitchen. There was no sink in the kitchen, no sink in the parlor either. All the washing up had to be done in the bathtub, which made it animal, vegetable and mineral when someone was trying to take a bath. There was no stove in the kitchen. Just an electric plate that overloaded the circuits and blew all the fuses.

When Simon had called the lack of sink to Mrs.

Mulcahy's attention, she had stared at him all milky, blue-eyed Irish incredulous.

"No sink? No sink at all," she had said. "Well, what will the landlords think of next, God love them."

"You'll mention it to the owners?" Simon had implored.

"Indeed I will," said Mrs. Mulcahy, "but landlords are all the same, the lot of them, God rest them."

It was Mrs. Mulcahy's fiction that there were "owners" and that she herself was only the superintendent, without power but with great compassion in her Celtic, bleeding-heart breast.

"Why won't she say she owns the house?" I whispered to Simon as we climbed and climbed the stairs to the artist's suite.

"She'd have to be responsible," Simon whispered back. "The Irish don't like to rule, you know, they only like to resist. Even when they have authority they must oppose themselves."

Mrs. Mulcahy opposed herself endlessly. There was never a day that went by that Mrs. Mulcahy did not have a complaint against the landlord. Not enough heat, too much heat. The pipes and drains wanted tending, the poor light on the stairs.

"No watt at all," she said with scorn and disdain. "It's only God's mercy none has fallen and broken a neck. If they do, they should sue the landlord and that's the truth." She paused; the enormity of her advice realized itself slowly. "Wait then," she said, tempering her first advice with prudence. "That would put you in the hands of the lawyers and you know what they are."

Mrs. Mulcahy found it necessary to get it into her head that I was Mr. Furtwangler's sister.

"Your sister's so pretty and such a darlin' girl. It's a fine thing her coming to see you so often. An actress, is she?"

Every day when there was no matinee, every day for the

two weeks we were in Boston, I went to climb Mrs. Mulcahy's stairs. Sometimes Simon came to meet me at the subway. Sometimes he ran in after me toting the green book bag stuffed with pâté and caviar and salami and black bread and the scrolls.

Simon was working on scrolls.

"Dead Sea Scrolls?" I asked.

"Well, old, certainly," Simon said with pride.

"What are they, then?"

"I won't know till I've translated them."

"When will that be?"

"When I crack the idiom, you idiot."

"When will that be?"

"I don't know," Simon said happily. "It's a lot of work, you know. I've had to learn a whole new alphabet, another language. I have the feeling these scrolls may be terribly important."

We hugged and hugged each other. How nice that we were both working so hard.

Every day was a party day. We stuffed ourselves with sweetmeats and napped and made love and napped again. I sat with Simon while he rolled and unrolled the scrolls. Then, when it was time for me to go, we got ourselves out of bed and took a bath together for the sheer joy of finding leftover green beans and brussels sprouts in the drain.

We lolled in the tub filled to the brim with hot water, foamed over all with a meringue of bubble bath, and waited for the vegetables to float to the top.

"Do you suppose," Simon sighed, "that the waters of the moon are as salubrious as the waters of the womb?"

There were complaints, of course. Undergraduates may entertain young women in their rooms but if they do they are never supposed to entertain them in the bathtub. We were undone.

It was not immorality that undid us so much as the bad

drains. The filling of the tub to the brim caused the leaking of the water on the ceiling below which caused the tenant below to complain to Mrs. Mulcahy.

"There now, and that's perfectly all right," snorted outraged Mrs. Mulcahy, "it's brother and sister they are."

But still and all the seed had been planted. Although Simon assured Mrs. Mulcahy that we were as pure as water could wash us, we were watched from that day on; from behind the lace curtains, from behind the newel post, from outside the attic door, we heard the rustle of little green-eyed mice. So it was just as well that the idyl was ending, that the show was moving toward New York and the opening.

"You'll come to the opening?" I asked Simon as I caught up handfuls of fluff in the tub. Simon sat at the other end, his back against the faucet knobs, his hair damp, plastered Caesar-like against his forehead as he watched his Cleopatra.

"Yes, I'll come," Simon said glumly.

"You don't sound very enthusiastic."

"You might as well know now," Simon was darkling and ominous, "Sidney and Shirley are coming, too."

"To the opening?"

"Yes."

"To see me?"

"Yes." Simon's eyes rolled up toward the bathroom ceiling in agony. No Roman bath had ever contained more blood than this. I began to laugh.

"They think you've been trapped by some old harridan of an actress, something with dyed hair and rough-raddled cheeks. They are coming to look me over and do me in."

Simon did not laugh. "Oh, my dear, my pretty, my sweet innocent. They are coming because they want to meet your mother. They hope they may lure her out for a champagne supper, tax deductible S & S Modes. They don't care if you have eaten me as long as they can name-drop your mother."

"That's all right, Simon," I said, patting his wet and naked chest with my wet and naked foot. "They can drink champagne out of Helen's slipper. I don't care as long as you come to my first Broadway opening. I need you, Simon, everybody needs a someone."

11

I NEEDED Simon a good deal more than I knew. The failure that had been put out of mind while we were all sleek and secure, with a paycheck every week, came to pass.

The failure was all the more cruel because on tour there had been an absence of real-life strains. Husbands, wives, children, mistresses all fade from view while actors are on tour. They live in theatres and hotel lobbies and steam-heated rooms. They are doing a job they like and that they are paid to do. They dress out of a suitcase and every once in a while, just for kicks, a trunk. They ring up room service for breakfast in bed. There is sometimes a vague sting of guilt that says they should eat stew instead of steak and save up something for that time when the tour is over. But they rarely do. No one believes the tour will ever end. They set up new domestic arrangements for the duration, they settle in for a new life in which one will always be twenty and live high off the hog.

Every member of that company should have had a fine old theatrical saying pinned to his underwear, "First in, first out." That's no more a true saying than any other theatrical bit of wisdom. But it was true for us. We were the first show of the season to open and the first show to close.

We opened on a Wednesday night. How it rained!

The opening-night audience was all friends or relatives

except for those dreadful, powerful seven men on the aisle. Still, friends and family could not fiddle up any enthusiasm. It had been dampened out of them before the curtain went up.

The Stage Society never gave opening-night parties or opening-night presents. Both meant giving away money and giving away money was against their religion.

After the curtain fell, Sidney and Shirley came backstage. Simon was holding them warily by their elbows. He looked like Dr. Jungle holding two vials of the virus that was killing him.

Sidney and Shirley insisted on taking us out: Mr. Margolies, Helen, Simon and me, and as a magnanimous afterthought, they included the playwright who sat whimpering in Helen's dressing room.

It seemed like a good idea to go with them because they were so hearty and affirmative. They were the only people saying kind and honeyed words to Helen or the playwright. All the rest was silence and lukewarm monkey vomit out of the mouths of strangers.

Sid and Shirl, as they insisted we call them, looked like they could take care of us and we needed a lot of tending.

The playwright was not really a dope fiend. It was not opium that made his pupils contract. It was fear. If he was not a success tonight, he had no place to go.

He had thrown up his teaching job at the Almond Academy the moment he received Helen's letter accepting his play. His ingenuous method of burning his academic bridges was to say something brief and Anglo-Saxon to the headmaster's wife. It was a place to which he could not return. It had, at any rate, been his last stop in a downhill teaching career. There would be no recommendation for him from the Almond Academy of Neosho, Missouri, and even if there were, there would be no place to send it.

He had counted on making his way in the theatre. He had

come East prepared to receive his rightful kingdom on Broadway. The only other job he'd ever had was waiting on tables to put himself through school. It was teach or write or back to the scullery. He snuggled up to Shirl. Tonight would be his last good meal before he was thrown back into that hell, the kitchen, to be forever bedeviled by the chef. The lack of applause had fractured his spirit. He had been scalded in live steam and hit with a hammer like a shattered clam. I could not bear to look at him or listen to his little bleats and whimpers.

Helen held herself regally upright, embalmed with the determination not to give way. She was dedicated to keeping an English stiff upper spine.

Mr. Margolies kept nervously circling her, trying to get in a position to catch her when she fell.

We sat in the ghastly light of an expensive supper club. The cornerstone of this restaurant's philosophy was that what is flambéed can be charged for twice over and if flambéed long enough, is almost unrecognizable. The waiters were, to a man, a group of gaudily uniformed northern Mediterranean pyromaniacs. They never stopped twirling flaming swords or heaving heated brandy into chafing dishes and tossing in a lighted match after it.

Simon had a lot to drink. He kept insisting he was a member of the Save the Brandy Foundation and it was his public and civic duty to keep brandy in its place in the stomach rather than in the frying pan.

Shirl ran a very long red fingernail up and down the playwright's arm. If there was a tiny spark of life still in him, she intended to find it and rekindle it.

Sid's opening gambit was patting. His great, hairy paw kept patting Helen on the back and on her hands which were placed carefully before her on the snow-white table-cloth. She looked like a medium about to go into a trance. Sid's pats were annoying her, keeping her from her other private world. She shrugged him off. He went underground and patted beneath the table. He got a paw on my knee and I gave a tiny, startled shriek.

"Sorry," he said most nicely and sincerely, "I thought it was your mother."

Shirl smiled. She had found a quivering nerve in the playwright's neck and was picking at it to her heart's content.

Simon began to sing very softly to himself looking a little like the Dormouse at the mad tea party. He sang a song of his own device, "While seated one day in a treacle well . . ." I wanted to tell them all that Simon never drank but all the phrases that went on and off neon-like in my head were of the "He's usually a most abstemious boy" variety.

Mr. Margolies tapped away at his water glass with a dull knife, saying over and over, "We must get your mother home before the notices come out. We must get your mother home before the notices come out."

Mr. Margolies was the hero of the hour. He had enough strength of character left to get up and get us out of the restaurant. It doesn't sound like Croix de Guerre work but medals should have been struck off for Mr. Margolies that night. He even paid the check.

We stood about in a clump on the sidewalk waiting to regroup into taxis, limousines and cars.

The playwright was remanded into the protective custody of the Furtwanglers. They had captured a live playwright. Shirl had him in her literal clutches. He sagged a bit but he was still edible. She had only to be patient and she could devour him tomorrow.

Sid had Helen's hand between his two furry mittens. He said, "Who the hell did that Bernhardt think she was? Can you answer me that?"

"No," Helen said, "no, no, no."

Simon disentangled himself from the leave-taking and began to wander away by himself into the night.

"Will you be all right?" I whispered.

"Oh, yes," he said. "I'm going to have a lovely, lovely sick and then I shall be quite all right."

Mr. Margolies was wise and valiant to get us away. The papers were brutal. They called an old hat an old hat. They said Helen's acting style just fitted under the old hat. They said her style might never come back but if it did, it must surely be in farce. They said the "little sacrifice" of the evening had been the unfortunate audience who had had to witness the exhibit. They told the daughter to be more careful in her choice of vehicles. They said the end of an era had come twice for the Hollywood star, once in movies and now on the stage.

The old family retainers were let off free. They were obviously much too good for their employer.

The playwright was skewered and toasted like a marsh-mallow over martyr's fagots. It was suggested that if he was going to copy other playwrights' work, he pick on one at a time and not take on a field that included such disparate types as Arthur Miller and Arthur Wing Pinero, George Bernard Shaw and George Ionesco.

"The only fresh, the only new thing in this whole very tired evening is Diana Bradon and she is on stage so briefly it's impossible to tell if she is really as fresh as she seems or whether it was the stale company she kept. Diana Bradon is something pleasant to look at in an evening of eyesores."

Helen didn't want to look at me. She couldn't stand the sight of me. I understood her feelings. If thy right hand offend thee, cut it off. If thy right eye offend thee, pluck it out. I was the rejected. Understanding does not make the hurt any the less. I felt I had no choice in the matter. I felt the rejected never did have the choice, only the rejecter.

For three weeks we had to go to the theater every day but Sunday and we went twice on Saturdays and Wednesdays. Can't you just see what a happy group we were? The audience was Stage Society Subscription and how they hated having tickets to a flop. The cast was surly and sullen. The stagehands missed all their cues and the prop man never washed the dishes.

I wish Helen had looked at me. Just once! I had a great need for a pat on the head. Instead I was put out by the scruff of my neck as though I had done something disgraceful on the carpet.

After the play closed, Helen took to her bed and had the blinds drawn. I saw clearly that Mr. Margolies did not expect Helen to come out until I had gone. Mr. Margolies may have thought Helen unfair, but as he said, "I don't like to see your mother so upset."

So without melodrama or even a farewell scene, I put my things in suitcases and boxes and I struck me out of Helen's life the way one would strike last week's set. But when I was ready to leave, I suddenly realized I had to have some place to go. I had never thought of that. Leaving home, putting all my things in a knapsack was a splendid gesture, but I didn't know where to take the things.

"Simon," I said on the telephone, "I'm leaving the parental roof. Do you know of an apartment, something I can afford?"

Long pause, some breathing and then, "How much can you afford?"

"I don't know. I've never handled money before." Like royalty.

"I'll call you back."

"Do that, Simon."

"What?"

"I'd rather not go to a hotel."

"Right, I'll call you back."

Simon called me back. It took him about twenty minutes in Cambridge to find me a flat in New York. Oh, that marvelous wonder-working man. He could fix anything.

"Diana?"

"Yes?"

"Simon."

"Yes?"

"I've got you an apartment."

"Oh, Simon."

"Cold water on Forty-fifth Street."

"The street of stars!"

"Après de Broadway, the boulevard of broken dreams."

"My name will be up in lights, Simon. You'll see, you'll see." Simon sighed.

"Do you want to know how much?"

"How much?"

"Twenty-seven-fifty."

"A week?"

"A month."

"Oh, Simon, magical you."

"Yes, I think so."

"Thank you."

"Any time. Any time."

And so I left Helen's house.

12

WHAT an apartment! The water wasn't cold but the apartment was. It was on the west side of Ninth Avenue, through an Alice in Wonderland rabbit-hole door, down a Kafka hall, across a Dublin courtyard, up four tenement flights, and there was seventh heaven.

It had two marvelous features. First feature: a fireplace with a teeny, tiny grate in which to burn cannel coal, if you had the price and the strength to get it up the four flights. Otherwise, heat was a kerosene stove but it smelled rather.

Second feature: a teeny, tiny closet, with a real toilet inside. Most cold-water flats had one toilet per floor and that was out in the hall. All this for twenty-seven-fifty. Even if I went to the laundromat every day and ate all my meals at l'automatique, I'd have money left over.

Simon came down on the weekend and climbed up the four flights, his green book bag over his shoulder. I hugged and kissed him like anything.

"Santa Claus is here! Santa Claus is here! What's for Christmas?"

"Lots and lots of figgy pudding," Simon said, "and a Happy New Year." He also had a good supply of tinned goodies from S. S. Pierce and his scroll.

"How's the scrollwork?"

"Coming — it's coming."

Simon had said the work he was doing was as hard as the cracking of Linear B and he had waited for me to be impressed. I would have been suitably impressed but I didn't know what Linear B was. I do know Simon worked at it like a tense beaver.

Simon came every weekend to get me tidied and organized. He did the cleaning and the marketing, he went to the laundromat and the cleaner, he went to the hardware for kerosene and the wood and ice man for the coal and betimes he worked at his scroll and loved it.

He took me to a play and out to supper and every Saturday night, Simon saw to it that I had a bath. He got me a nice tin tub from the local hardware. We put it in the other room — the one that didn't have the fireplace. Simon covered the walls round with oilcloth and he said I was to pretend I was in Paris. Simon boiled up a lot of water either too hot or too tepid but he always put a surprise in the tub to ease the pain.

The first time it was a carnation — quite green.

"Not as original as string beans," said Simon, "but I had a lot of trouble getting it — it not being Saint Paddy's Day and all. I do think Oscar would have been wild to miss this flat."

Simon even looked behind my ears to see if I was dry. Simon was a very good mother to me. After the bath, we lay on the unfurled hide-a-bed and cuddled like Hansel and Gretel by the light of the cannel coal. Simon would move his finger across the chicken tracks of his scroll and I would babble on about the forest of producers I had tried to see the week before.

I was on my own now to make my way in society. Doesn't making one's way in society summon up pictures of charity balls, worthwhile teas, fittings at Mainbocher's and being photographed for the *Times* above caption "Ladies Meet to Discuss Benefit"?

My society was made up of all the lost boys and girls from all the unhappy nurseries all over the country, dedicated to the proposition of never growing up, determined to make their stars shine bright in the heaven of never-never land.

Most of them existed in cold-water walkups on peanut butter and the casting news. They paid their way with part-time jobs and handouts from home. They kept their Dionysian fires alight in acting classes. They kept each other company by the shoal like itty-bitty fishes in the big cold pond of Broadway.

The society was close. We were all the brothers, sisters, fathers, mothers, friends and lovers denied to us in every other society. It takes one to know one — we all recognized each other instantly. Much better than apprentae were we. The apprentae were only quasi-outs who could always write home that they were on the way and please kill the fatted calf. They had been pretentious frauds who would sooner or later defect to the marketplace of their fathers. The apprentae had been Rotarian in contrast to the outgroup of my new society.

The society of the theatre in all times, in all countries, in all languages, is made up of only two kinds of people, the people you want and the people who want you. If more people want you than you want you are one big success and you are in.

If you want more people than want you, you are one big failure and you are out.

Nobody wanted any of us, we were all way out there trying to get in. Since no one else wanted us, we wanted each other all the more. Since no one else would see us, we saw each other all the time. All through the night we talked the game we were not allowed to play and we took classes.

Our teacher was an out-of-work actor who had worked once and might work again. He dropped the names of the great and the near-great like pearls before uncultured swine.

76

He knew all the names because he had been in and among them once — had been found wanting — and was now out trying to get in again.

We worked on scenes and some got so hung up on scenes, they could never do a whole play again. We had been in plays before in college, high school, and community groups. Once again I was elite because I had had a real part in a real play.

This angered our guru. He spent a lot of time in class cutting me up to a smaller size. He said one of the worst things that could happen to an actor was to appear before he was prepared, *An Actor Prepares* being the title of the great book on acting. Some thought that was all there was to it and went on and on preparing forever. They grew old preparing but were never ready.

The object of the game is something else again. The object of the game is to, ready or not, act upon the stage.

Simon said those were truths he held to be self-evident. Simon didn't fit in with the actors' group, he was too interested in his scroll life to pay much attention to ego-deficient runaways.

When they asked Simon what he thought of their performance in a scene at the workshop, he was liable to say, "What scene?" Then, while they were still gasping like fish on the shore, Simon would begin to lecture them on Linear B, Ancient Persian, the Essenes and the possibility that his scroll which had been found in Ethiopia was in some way connected with a pre-Christian sect who believed they had the Messiah in their midst and had been so dismayed at His presence and perfection that they had killed Him. Simon said he believed man would always kill Christ. He said the word made flesh would have to be destroyed by man because man was so far from the life lived in love. Simon said a lot about his scrolls. My dear little acting friends were made nervous by Simon. He seemed to them to be a complete civilian. So I kept Saturdays and Sundays for Simon alone. Besides, the chores had to be done sometime.

Between classes, talking all the night through with out-of-work actors, and Simon for the weekend, I managed to get about and leave my name, my picture, and my aura in producers' offices.

Not very easy because any office that's producing is too busy casting to see actors and any producer that is not producing doesn't need to see actors. There's never a time that's right to call.

Agents are worse; they have to sell brand names. Brand X has no commercial value. It's hard enough to push a nationally advertised product.

The only people who see actors are casting directors because they must see someone sometime or lose their identities. They may see new faces but they cast old ones. Not that I blame them. They hire the sure, safe, predictable performance they have hired before. Money, not the muse, is riding on the production. If they are choosy and rejective, it's because they have a recurrent occupational nightmare in which they have just picked a lemon in the garden of Thespis. It's hard enough even in these times when you're insured against total failure by a million-dollar advance to make a modest success.

But every year, someone, somehow, breaks through. Someone gets propelled over from one whirling wheel within a wheel to another whirling wheel nearer the center. That center that all the peripheral people believe to be the dry eye of the storm, the King's cross, steadied by the gyroscope of reputation already made.

From where they are at the far edge of the centrifugal Siberia, they cannot see that there in the dead center those who seem to be standing still and imperturbable in attitudes of greatness are really hanging on for dear life while they pray Tibetian wheels full of prayers that there is no more room at the top; that they have got the last seat in the lifeboat; that they are never going to die and that if they do by some mischance pass over they will take their hard-earned place with them.

So I went around and around and knocked on doors and did scenes in class and looked for my chance to advance to a circle a little closer to that center, no matter how unsound and precarious it might really be.

I wanted to get there, and to get there I had to have a part upon the stage and getting a part seemed very difficult indeed. The worst thing next to having no experience at all was to have had a part in a flop. Failure sticks like anything and the odor of Helen clung.

It would be a lie to say I did not get in any doors. Because I was Helen and Brandon's daughter, I got in to see old friends, old enemies and the curious. They were all full of useless advice and of no help at all.

And then I got a job! Not because I was pretty or talented or had push or had pull, but because I had a little luck and I was in the right place at the right time. Isn't it funny about time? That's the coming dimension to watch.

For all those weeks I had wandered from door to door, beat my head against the walls and wailed from the wilderness without and then there I stood in an agent's office — the agent had a telephone, it rang. Someone on the other end wanted an actress and the agent sent me over to the Morocco Theatre to read.

There I went, out on the empty work-lit stage, and I read. When I had finished, the producer, Jimmie Dundee, came out of the dark house and looked up at me as I stood all white and trembling. He smiled.

"Nice reading, we'll let you know."

I smiled, frozen with fright and fear of failure.

"Thank you," I said and I ran away, my heart beating and my ears ringing. The next day was Thanksgiving.

Simon and I had it together in the cold-water flat. Helen wasn't up to turkey, she'd had hers for the year. Sidney and Shirley took the playwright to Florida for his. He had stayed on with them ever since the opening, a sort of Seventh Avenue court jester. He was working on a biography of the S & S Modes, a romance of labor, sweated and unionized. He was also entertaining Shirley along the way.

So Simon and I had the little fall festival to ourselves. He had gone to Chambord and had them put us up a hamper of duck and brandied cherries, wild rice and such. He had brought trinkets in the green book bag — dried corn, shellacked gourds, a horn of plenty.

We ate high off the canard, grew tipsy on the cherries and Simon read aloud from Herrick and Hopkins, I liking the Herrick better.

Then the phone rang.

"Hello."

"Diana Bradon?"

"Speaking."

"Jimmie Dundee."

"Hello, Jimmie Dundee," a little flippant for courage.

"You read for me yesterday."

"True." Pause.

"We're going into rehearsal Monday." More pause from me.

"Lovely for you."

Jimmie Dundee laughing. "Lovely for you too if you want a job."

I began to make a little sound over and over, "Oh, oh, oh . . ."

"It's a small part," Jimmie Dundee said still laughing, "but I think you can make it count." I reached out for Simon.

"Oh, oh."

"Would you like to talk about the part?"

"Yes. When?"

"What about now, say in an hour. Meet me at Sardi's."

"Now?"

"Why not?"

"I've got someone here — a guest." I was still holding tight to Simon. Long pause.

"Well, then some other time."

"When?"

Jimmie Dundee laughed right out loud, "Sometime soon."

"All right." What had I said that was so funny?

"I'll see you Monday."

"At rehearsal?"

"At rehearsal. Well, goodbye and a Happy Thanksgiving."

"Goodbye. Oh, wait, please wait."

"I'm still here," Jimmie Dundee said.

"Thank you."

"Quite all right," and he hung up.

It was Thanksgiving, Thanksgiving, Thanksgiving! Simon did not like the sound of it.

"You know what they say about Jimmie Dundee?"

"No, what do they say about Jimmie Dundee?"

"They say he eats virgins and spews out their bones."

"Well then, since I'm not a virgin it won't be a problem, will it?" Simon blushed and his jaw set.

"All right, have it your own way, but Jimmie Dundee is trouble. Not for nothing is he known as the Jolly Lecher."

"Did it ever occur to you," I asked huffily, "that he might think I'm the best for the part?"

"Come off it," Simon said and he made a very rude noise.

"Don't spoil it for me, Simon, please don't."

"Don't spoil it for yourself."

I shivered.

"What's the matter?" Simon asked.

"Nothing," I said, "nothing at all."

13

THERE was a cold snap. We ran out of wood, we ran out out kerosene, we drank too much wine, we lost our appetites and the mice came in droves to eat the crumbs.

I minded the mice. It was all very well to say it was only the two bad mice and that one always bought a little something extra for Tom Thumb and Hunca Munca, his wife. But there were more than two and when I was alone, when Simon was at school, when it was cold and dark and I was lost away from my mother, I could hear them pittering and pattering and rustling in the wastepaper basket. I never really saw their eyes glowing in the dark but that was because I put my head under the covers and shut my eyes tight enough to see green and yellow pinwheels instead.

Simon lectured me severely on the way of the flesh, sin, lust, chastity, honor, virtue, and then packed up his bag and scroll and went back to school Sunday morning instead of Sunday night because Monday I was going to rehearsal and I had to wash my hair and he was in it.

Monday was lovely. My lucky agent had gotten me ten dollars over minimum. We read through the first act in the morning. Jimmie Dundee sent out to the Gaity Delicatessen for sandwiches and we all ate lunch together. We read the second and third acts in the afternoon. I got two laughs and Jimmie Dundee took me to dinner at Sardi's. He made me laugh more than twice. He fed me cannelloni, fruit cup and espresso. Jimmie Dunee did not rape me, proposition me, or squeeze my knee. We sat drinking coffee for me and stingers for Jimmie Dundee until the supper crowd came in. Jimmie Dundee sent me home by myself in a taxi unviolated or sexually tampered with in any way. I had laughed until I was tired enough to sleep without thinking about the mice.

Jimmie Dundee was a very funny man. All his audiences knew it. Jimmie Dundee had been around the business a long time and he had always made them laugh. He could say "Your mother's dead" or read from the yellow pages and make them laugh.

It was also said he had made half the female population of Actors' Equity, although some felt that to be a conservative estimate. Whatever the actual figures, he had always made the ladies laugh. There were no hard feelings, all was done in the spirit of comedy. He always left them laughing. No suicides, no divorces, no abortions, no bastards. If there was an occasional tear, it was quickly dried. He was the wonder of the world.

Jimmie could be seen any day in the week, having lovely gossip and giggles with a tableful of old flames who were all now nicely banked to an old-school-tie glow.

Jimmie had made movies but they failed to catch him in the magic box. He had had a television series which ran for the thirteen weeks and out. Jimmie was not for the tube. Jimmie had been on radio but Jimmie was not for the ears alone. Jimmie Dundee was a round actor born for the stage and live audiences who liked to laugh.

He had been a "Tennis anyone" juvenile. He had been a "Monica, I love you terribly" young leading man. He had been a second-billing "We've been married ten years and you're lovelier than ever" co-star. He had been the father "I wish we had had this talk sooner" of an adolescent daughter. He had been the old roué next door; "I think you've made the right decision with the wrong man" who loved but lost the virgin heroine. He had been the only star in a play with three small boys and a dog. "The one that barks is my son." And he had made them laugh. If there was a laugh there, he'd get it. If there wasn't one there, he'd get it.

Jimmie went over the script with me. My part was almost as small as the one in Helen's play. But it was spread out so I came on in every act. Jimmie Dundee said I had three show-stopping laughs and one exit hand. I said he was crazy but I said it to myself.

It was Jimmie Dundee's play first to last. It was Jimmie Dundee's tour of duty as a world-weary mystery writer who gets mixed up with an international spy ring. Every time the plot thickened or grew silly, I came on as a sort of sight gag. The girl in the peekaboo hat. Jimmie Dundee taught me to get on, get my laugh and get off the stage. Never once did he pinch, pant or breathe down my neck. But all the same, I knew Simon was right. In the parlance of Broadway, Jimmie Dundee was trouble waiting to happen. Mr. Dundee and I had an obligatory scene to play.

We were to open cold in town, a week of paid previews and then the critics. That meant there wasn't much time for slaps and tickles. Jimmie Dundee had lots of his own money in this one. He was also the co-producer. He really directed although there was a man of that title who sat smoking a cigar and saying "That's great" to the company from time to time. The director and Jimmie had worked together before. He thought Jimmie was as funny as everyone else. Most of the cast had played with Jimmie before. The leading lady had played with him on and off. She adored him. She brought her children to the first run-through. They were crazy about Jimmie, as were her husband, her maid, her press agent, and her accountant.

With all that laughing and giggling and hugging and

kissing and general jollity, it seemed a shame to break up the fun and games and bring the audience into it. The old gang had taken me into the fold, no pecking order to nag me now. I was new but I would do.

The playwright was English. He came over for rehearsals. Jimmie had Americanized the script and the playwright thought what Jimmie had done was wizard. No fear-crazed eyes, no seedy suits, no throwing up in the men's room. The playwright laughed all the day through and at least once a day he pointed at me and said, "There's the girl in the peekaboo hat," and the whole company fell apart.

It sounds simpleminded but that's all there was to it. The night of the dress rehearsal I got the hat, a lot of feathers and bows and organdy ruffles and ribbons. Such a silly hat! Everyone thought it was fine. It fit. When the audience saw it, they thought it was fine, too. A week of previews and I got every laugh and my exit hand.

Opening night all those famous, in-the-know, couldn't-be-wrong people liked Jimmie Dundee, the play, and they liked me. No tears, no failure, just roars and roars of laughter and a party at Sardi's to look forward to.

When it's a hit, bunches of people climb to the third tier of dressing rooms to see the bit players. They crowd in all "darlings" and "marvelous" and "you were divines" just on the off chance you may remember they were there at the moment of truth.

My dressing room was small and they were many. I had presents and flowers and loads of wires. Brandon was proud of me in ten words. Mr. Margolies had sent flowers with Helen's name on them. Simon's present was a big box of mousetraps and a little ivory mouse.

I had not seen Simon since Thanksgiving. We had put forth some pretty euphemisms about being busy. We had talked on the phone, remote communiqués from two polar expeditions, one at the North Pole, one at the South.

Because of the time difference of our lives, there was never a call that was convenient, too early in the day for me, too late for him. All the exchanges had been very much the same.

"Hello, Diana?"

"What?" Asleep.

"Diana?"

"Who?" Still asleep.

"CI 6–7857?"

"Yes." Waking up.

"Simon here."

"Oh, Simon, hello, Simon." Awake.

"Are you asleep?"

"No!" Indignant.

"It's nearly noon."

"We had a late rehearsal."

"Oh?"

"The whole company — very late."

"How's the weather?"

"Cold. How's the weather there?"

"Cold."

"How's the scroll?"

"OK."

"Making any progress?"

"None. Can't tell if it's left to right or right to left."

"Don't give up."

"I won't. How's the play?"

"OK."

"Getting your laughs?"

"I try."

"Don't give up."

"Anything special you want, Simon?"

"No."

"OK. Call me soon, Simon."

"Sure."

There was no room for Simon in my dressing room. He

stood out in the hall trying to keep out of harm's way. Jimmie Dundee rushed in, one big grin.

"I adore you. Wear your hat to the party." I said I would. He gave me a huge hug. I saw Simon's face over Jimmie's shoulder.

"May I bring a friend to the party?" Jimmie turned and saw Simon, a bigger grin.

"By all means," he said. "Bring your young man." And he was gone.

Simon was dark and silent. The dressing room was empty now but Simon would not come in.

"Sorry to be so long, Simon."

"OK, OK."

"I loved your present."

"You're a big hit."

"Are we?"

"A big success."

"Oh, Simon, truly?"

"Success to all successful thistle sifters." I put on my hat, it was very silly.

"Three thousand thistles," I said.

"Through the thick of my thumb," said Simon.

"Don't they hurt?" I asked Simon as I closed the dressing room door.

"Only when I laugh," Simon said.

I took Simon's hand and dragged him along after me; big crush on the stairs, at the stage door. Strangers in the theatre alley saying "There she is, the one in the hat."

Broken-field running across Forty-fifth Street dodging the taxis and the crowd in Shubert Alley. A montage of New Year's Eve and the Armistice being signed. Other shows letting out, real working actors saying, "Hear you're a hit. You'll run for a year." Dodging the taxis on Forty-fourth Street and then try to get into Sardi's. Scenes from the

Russian Revolution, Eisenstein's best. The famine in *The Good Earth.*

"Let them through. Can we get a table? Do you have a reservation?" Then Jimmie Dundee had me by the elbow.

"Make way for the girl in the peekaboo hat." He got me through the mob past the velvet rope, me clinging to Simon for dear life. In we went to cries of "Vivat Regina," to the assembled jury of my peers.

Not much for a real queen. A bunch of tatty players in a small café, but when you're eighteen and want it so, it makes up for every other year of your life. It makes the eyes to sparkle and tear. It makes one to drink champagne and to love everybody, just everybody.

"You've had enough champagne."

"Who says?"

"Simon says."

"I want some more champagne."

"Time to go home."

"Don't want to go home."

"Have to go home."

"Afraid to go home."

"Why?"

"Mice."

"Little mice."

"Big mice."

"Mice won't hurt you."

"They read."

"Mice can't read."

"Can read. Get in my wastebasket and read my mail." I began to cry.

"Homesville."

I sobbed.

"What's the matter?"

"My hat. I've lost my hat. Where's my hat?"

"It's on your head."

"Oh."

14

WHEN I woke up my category had been changed. The notices were raves. Jimmie Dundee had done it again. I had been singled out for honorable mention. I had been swept several whirling circles away from the society of the poor and the needy, the shy and the shoddy. I was not a star in the safe center or anything near it, but I was "The Girl in the Peekaboo Hat." I was now well into the circle of the sleek and the sly, the witty and the wicked, in which everybody had a warm coat for the winter and an analyst of their own.

I also woke up with a hangover. My poor melon head rested on Simon. He had managed to get me into the hide-a-bed minus hat and dress and shoes but plus slip and all that lay beneath it. I knew Simon was already awake, lying there for my convenience; not moving so as to let me rest peacefully for as long as I could before I had to face real life. I said, "If you sleep with me, Simon, you'll have to marry me."

"If I marry you," Simon said, "I'd have to sleep with you."

I started to cry.

"Oh, my God," Simon said, "this is where we left off last night. Have you any idea how long it took me to get you to dry up and stop that bawling?"

I wailed. "You're not my buddy chum pal anymore."

"Yes, I am," Simon said. "I'm your very best friend in all the whole wide world. I read you all your lovely notices," and he patted me.

"Don't touch me," I snuffled. Snuffling made my head hurt all the more. "You're too perfect for me. All this 'Oh, what a friend you have in Jesus' life is giving me a pain."

"Just guilt," Simon said trying to move me off him. I clutched at him wetly and wildly. "If you'll let me go," Simon said, "I'll make you some coffee."

"Instant or regular?"

"Regular."

I let him go. I did not want to think of guilt. Christmas was coming, the geese were getting fat. I wanted to buy a little brown coat and a fur muff and hat to match and I wanted to go live in a toy department. Maybe not a department, maybe a whole toy store like F. A. O. Schwartz.

"What are you going to give me for Christmas, Simon?"

"A hard time," Simon said, "if you don't shape up and stop lusting after that jolly lecher you're working for."

"Unfair," I cried, "and falsely accused."

"Oh, come off it." Simon was making a lot of racket with cups and saucers and pots and pans. He was very upset.

"Why are you so upset?"

"I'm not."

"You are."

"Cream and sugar?"

"Black."

"Listen, Simon." I sat up and pulled the covers around me to give me strength and to keep me warm.

"I'm listening."

"Are you going to marry me?"

"Nope."

"Never?"

"Never." The cold was everywhere. It would take more than blankets to keep me warm.

"Why not?" I wished I had three wishes and all of them would be for Simon to marry me.

"I told you once, don't make me tell you again. I'm mortally wounded, blighted, ruined."

"No, you're not. You are wonderful, Simon. Why do you think you're ruined?"

"Maybe it's because I saw something nasty when I was a child."

"What did you see?"

"Sidney and Shirley."

"Listen, Simon, listen. You'll change. You'll see. A few more years at the analyst and you'll be as good as new."

"Oh, dear," Simon said sadly. He had brought the coffee on a tray. He sat on the side of the bed while he drank it. "You're looking for a miracle. I don't think I exist. I think I'm no one. If I don't find something to do, a job, a title of something I am doing and that I am, there isn't anyone there for you to marry."

"Don't miracles happen?" I pleaded.

"Yes," Simon said, "but not very often."

"Well then, I'll look for a miracle. To me Simon, you are. You take care of me. You do care for me. I know that. Everything in this apartment is you. You are where I live."

"Yes," said Simon, his face all twisted up in pain as if I had stuck a knife in him and twisted it around. "I care for you. You are real. You are working but I'm just someone who's waiting for something to happen."

"But in analysis, if you can find out what your problem is you can do something about it, can't you?"

"Why is it," Simon said softly, "that people think the blind don't know they can't see?"

"What?"

"My problem can't be helped. It's an irreparable loss. I'm the blind eye of love. And so are you. We're blighted beyond repair."

"I don't know what you mean."

"You mean you don't want to know," Simon said, "but it's true all the same. We're little freaks who ought to be put on view for the public good. A sort of warning to all the peoples of the earth. If you abuse the heart generation after generation, you get us, the loveless ones."

"Not me, Simon. Not me. I'm not loveless. I love you, Simon, I do."

I pushed the tray away and upset the coffee cup. The coffee spattered on the comforter making brown stains that would never wash out. We dabbed at the spots with our paper napkins and they turned brown and soggy.

"Illusion, lovey." Simon took the tray and put it on the floor. "You're living an illusion of love."

"You speak for yourself, Simon. I love you but if you won't love me, don't tell me I'm loveless. I'm not a freak. I'm full of love. I'm going to love someone and live happily ever after. I'm going to have sixteen children and love them terribly."

"Just like Helen and Brandon."

"No, just like me."

"You'll never make it."

"Shut up."

"Never in a million years."

"Shut up!"

"Don't try it, let it go." Simon was shaking me by the shoulders. "Let it go. You've got your work. Take your blessing and be grateful for it." I hit out against him.

"You shut up, Simon. You go away and leave me alone. If you won't let me love you, I'll go and love the Jolly Lecher." Simon let me go. He picked up the tray and stood with it over my head.

"God pity you. What a pail of Italian garbage you've picked to wallow in."

"I wouldn't wallow if you loved me enough to keep me from it." Simon turned away.

"Where are you going?"

"I'm going to get a piece of paper and a pencil," Simon said.

"Why, why?"

"I'm going to write 'I will not say I told you so' five hundred times."

15

I WALLOWED in more than garbage. I was the complete
comedy of errors. All was vanity under my sun. There
was nothing new in it but it was all new to me. I waded in
grinning like a fool — I just loved it when people said,
"There goes the girl in the peekaboo hat."

The audience began to chant it whenever I came on for a
curtain call. Comedians on television took it up as a word
and sight gag. Taxi drivers nearly drove into lampposts as
they turned to stare. "Hey, ain't you the girl in the peekaboo
hat?" I was photographed and paragraphed; I was the mystery guest on *What's My Line?*

I moved out of the mouse palace into a theatrical hotel.
Sitting room and bedroom and kitchenette just big enough
to shake up a Scotch sour in. I entertained and was entertained. I met everyone and everyone met me. Jimmie
Dundee put me on public view — Exhibit A. It was taken
for granted that we were sleeping together. Being caught by a
Journal-American photographer dazed-eyed behind a Stork
Club ash tray was tantamount to being caught in flagrante
delicto.

I went Christmas shopping every moment I had off from
the whirling wheel. I found me that little brown coat and
muff and hat. It seemed to me it was my season and that
every light in the city was shining for me alone. The tree in
Radio City was put up only for my pleasure.

I was a creature of conditioned response. Every time I thought of Jimmie Dundee, I thought of hugs and kisses I associated with delicious success. I smelled tweed and cigarette smoke with a dash of peppermint. He drank a bit, you see, and didn't want to offend.

But every time I thought of Simon, I winced for the shame of being rejected. I felt the kiss of betrayal. I closed my eyes and it was cold and the mice ran everywhere until at last they were broken in a trap.

I told myself I loved my new life. It was, or so it seemed to me, a vast improvement over my old one. But Helen disagreed. On Christmas Eve, Helen sent for me. I was summoned to her pink chamber. I went willingly, hopefully. I ran all the way through the carolers, the shoppers, the falling snow. I thought she had a present for me. We played out our nativity scene. It was a scene that never should have been staged. It surely was far from obligatory. It was my fault, I accept the guilt. I should have known from the start how near the edge Helen was. All she needed was one small shove and over she'd go. She served me a cup of tea from her high-tea table, but she began in the accusative case, all puckered-up brow and pursed-up lip.

"You're making a display of yourself," Helen said. Not "How do you do, my darling daughter," or a "Merry Christmas all." My adrenalin flowed, the hackles, whatever they may be, went up; I rejoined in bellus defensive, rattling my tea cup in its saucer.

"In what way, pray?" In that instant an experienced player could have told from the dialogue how badly it was going to end.

"All this going about in a hat!" Helen's hands floundered in my direction.

"That's my job."

"Exploitation. Why don't you wear a signboard on you, front and back."

95

"At least I've got something to advertise."

"What's that supposed to mean?" Helen had smelled blood and her nostrils quivered.

"I'm working." No subtle torture for me, just one big turn of the rack and crunch, there go the bones. But once you get a taste of cruelty, it's hard to give up such a sweet cup. Helen went white.

"You might think about your name. Did you ever? Brandon and I have made something of ourselves. We have a right to be proud."

"Are you saying I'm a disgrace?"

"You're on your way."

"Thank you. Thank you very much."

"What you're doing is not acting, it's only a cheap display." Helen had a lot of courage. She sat up straight on the pink chaise and looked me in the eye. I looked her back.

"What is it you want, Helen? Do you want me to be a really fine actress like you?" Helen shriveled up. The air went out of her; she got smaller and smaller and floated away like my balloons used to do at the park zoo. I reached out to her to try to get her back but I only burned my hand on the spirit lamp under the tea kettle.

They say you forget the unpleasant things. That's not true. You blot out the nice and the good but you keep the horrid right around the corner all spruced up ready to trot it out anytime when it's evening and you have no home or you have a cold or you're growing a little older. Any Sunday afternoon when you wake up from a nap and don't know where you are or even if you're still alive.

I was sorry the minute I had said it but done was done and no way back to where we had been before. I managed to get out of the apartment and to the theatre for the matinee. Wouldn't you know it would be a matinee day? My hand was badly burned. I did not know what to do for it.

I cried in my dressing room where Jimmie Dundee found

me and cosseted me and kissed away my tears. I was hungry for cosseting and Jimmie Dundee was an old China hand at that kissing. I'll still say that for him any day. One error leads to another. That's something else I'll still say any day.

Of course it didn't seem like error at the time or I wouldn't have done it. At the time it was honeymoon hill and just what I deserved for having had such a mean mummy and daddy all my young years.

I had been starving for affection, hungering for warmth. Jimmie Dundee was my sunshine, my only sunshine. I only had eyes for him. Night and day, he was the one for me. I had found him just in time.

But after we had sung all those old songs, we had to settle down and jog along together. Nobody could keep up that kind of caterwauling day in, day out, besides Jimmie Dundee was growing long in the tooth. Once the edge was off the appetite, it didn't seem to be a very satisfactory meal after all. If that sounds cold-blooded, the blood is very often cold after the fact. While it had lasted, we had had a feast of the flesh. We had nibbled and munched and gnawed away at each other insatiable in our effort to derive a little nourishment from the arrangement. It was Christmas and I had gotten my just desserts.

Just after the first of the new year, Helen was taken off to a rest home in Connecticut. A very rich, very quiet, organ-in-the-billiard-room sort of place. A converted mansion that made it seem as if going mad was quite the nicest thing really nice people could do. Tea on the lawn when the weather was fine or if the weather looked chancy, tea in the library by the fire. Helen was not really mad, she was just tired and in need of a little rest. When she felt better, she'd love to see me. She spoke of me often and always kindly, Mr. Margolies called to tell me. He said he knew I'd want to know.

Mother was in the laughing academy but the jokes were not over.

97

Jimmie Dundee and I had to find something to talk about until it was lunchtime again. We began to talk about him. He was really very serious, very spiritual. Maybe he was laughing on the outside but he was crying on the inside. He was very sad. He was very sad because he understood his wife and she understood him.

I was glad he was not misunderstood as well as sad. He had been married to his wife for more years than I had been alive. Perhaps if they had had a child, they would not have been sad. They had no children but they had dogs. Jimmie Dundee looked happier when he talked about his dogs.

They were Corgis. Jimmie Dundee said Corgis were miles beyond any other breed and his Corgis were champions. Not that there weren't problems. You had to watch their diet or they put on weight. One extra dog biscuit and pow. Then too, there was the problem of wax in their ears. Corgis had acute hearing and you had to watch out for wax. Things like wax and diet and exercise and grooming for show could keep Jimmie Dundee talking almost all the night.

Jimmie Dundee had a walletful of pictures. His favorite dog was named Elf. Elf was getting on a bit but she was just as alert as ever. She'd thrown many a good litter. One national champion was her son. Her last litter had been by Caesarean. For a while it had been nip and tuck. Jimmie Dundee said he didn't know what he'd do if anything ever happened to Elf.

Not that he didn't like Baron Rothschild and Minnie Mouse. But Elf was his favorite. Elf had his heart.

We settled into a routine, as I suppose all couples do. Sunday, Tuesday and Friday nights he spent at home. Monday, Wednesday, Thursday and Saturday were all mine. I certainly had the lion's share although I began to wonder if he would rather not be out walking the dogs instead of in amusing me.

We went on our petty pace till nearly spring and then one

Monday night as we sat in my theatrical hotel drinking cocoa and looking at the dog breeder's manual, in walked his wife.

One had been prepared for such an eventuality by novels and movies, books and plays. The confrontation scene. I had hoped when it came to me, I should play it through with dignity. It had never occurred to me, and I have to laugh when I think of it even now — it had never occurred to me he might, if given a choice, choose his wife instead of me. Actually he didn't have to choose between his wife and me. No such choice was offered. It was no two-party system, this election.

When she walked in, Jimmie looked up, pale and shaken as one might well imagine and then he shook himself together and said, "What's the matter? What's wrong?" An odd question if you think about it. But she didn't think it odd. They communicated beautifully.

"It's Elf," she said to Jimmie. She never looked at me. "Elf's dead."

"Oh, my God," said Jimmie Dundee. He put his head in his hands and his shoulders shook.

His wife cradled him to her flat chest and let him mourn.

"There, there," she kept saying, "there, there." Jimmie finally got himself together.

"When did Elf — go?"

"About an hour ago." His wife smoothed back his receding hair from his forehead.

"Was she in pain?" Jimmie asked.

"No, none," his wife said. "Now come away, do, you'll want to see her before they come from the dog mortuary."

Jimmie nodded dumbly.

He got his coat; she helped him put it on.

I couldn't help asking, it was so much on my mind.

"How," I asked Jimmie, "did your wife know where to find you?"

"Oh," Jimmie said in a daze, "I told her where I'd be in

case Elf needed me. Elf's been ill for some time and with Corgis you never know."

"No," I said, "you never know."

"Where's my hat?" Jimmie asked piteously.

"Here's your hat," I said. "Now what's your hurry?"

16

THE show was canceled for three performances while Jimmie Dundee laid Elf to rest. I took the time off to go up to Boston to see Simon. Perhaps, if I made my confession to him, he would know what penance I must do for my sins. I was indeed growing up. I now had some guilt of my own. My life was beginning to be a burden I could not carry. While looking for my true love I had been picked up by the master of the hounds.

It gave me a queer feeling to be running up the stairs to Mrs. Mulcahy's attic suite. What would the Garden of Eden look like to Eve after the fall? We had played so happily there before I had begun my foolish games of serpents and apples.

Simon opened the door and stood looking at me in silence. I was afraid he might not let me in.

"Are you burning the midnight oil?" I asked nervously.

"Well, it's that or set fire to oneself," Simon said, still not moving.

"Feeling like a martyr?"

"A bit, yes." Simon stared at me. I could not go on meeting his eyes; I hung my head.

"Let me in, Simon, do!"

Simon stood aside and let me in. His work was spread out all over every table, chair and bureau. The scroll magnified, reduced, in fragments, reproduced by machine and by hand, now occupied Simon's whole space on earth.

"You're going to a lot of trouble for one old scroll," I said in what I hoped was a light voice.

"Well, they went to a lot of trouble to dig it up. There's always the chance it may be the answer to all mankind's problems. Perhaps it's the wisdom and the way we're looking for."

"Do you know what it says?"

"Not yet." I waited but Simon was silent, so I had to begin.

"I really didn't come to discuss your work." My face felt as stiff and unnatural as the words.

"I can see that. Do you think you're in shock?"

"I don't know."

"I think perhaps you are. Your eyes don't seem to track. I'll make you a milk food drink and get you a hot brick." Simon really seemed to be very concerned.

"I think I'd like to sit down," I said weakly.

"Yes, do." Simon made a place for me in a chair. He went away and presently he came back with a glass of hot milk and brandy.

"Here, drink this."

I drank and felt the warmth I had been so long without. Simon kept on looking and looking. Finally, when he had seen enough, he shook his head.

"Well, it's happened I see and I cannot help saying, I told you so."

"Do forbear, Simon."

"All right, I won't say it," Simon said. "But I shall think it all the same. I suppose you've come to tell me all."

"Yes."

"Oh, Lord, I was afraid so."

"I must tell. If I keep it to myself, I'll die of it."

"Then tell," Simon said wearily.

"There's not much to tell," I began piteously. "I just seem to have gone to the dogs." My confession and the brandy struck me funny. I was full of merriment and began to laugh until the tears flooded down my face. "Oh, Simon," I said, "I do want to get out of this pail of garbage but it's a bit deeper than just having eaten a piece of flesh that didn't agree with me. If that were all, I should simply say I'm not a very good cannibal and forget it, but there's more. I've not honored my father, let alone my mother. You see, Simon," I paused for effect, "quite calmly and with malice afore-thought, I pushed Helen into a pit." Simon looked surprised.

"Can you be sure?" he asked very seriously.

"Well, she's gone."

"No, no." Simon was impatient. "Can you be sure you are at fault? Don't you think she was ready to go over the edge anyway?"

"True, Simon, but she was still on the edge. I pushed her over."

"Yes," Simon agreed, "you must accept that much."

"What must I do, Simon? There must be some way to forget it?"

Simon shook his head. I think he said sternly, "You're looking for an easy and absolute end to your little trans-gressions."

"They don't seem little to me." How could Simon believe I did not regard my lapses from grace with the great defer-ence they deserved?

"Well, they are little," Simon said, "whether you think it now or not. It's the easy and the absolute that are large matters."

"Are you making fun of me, Simon?" Simon smiled and gave me a maddeningly paternal pat.

"Not at all, although you must admit you've been taking part in the human comedy." I gave a cry of agony. Simon saw he had gone past my comprehension.

"There, there," he said, "there, there."

"You must do better than that," I snapped. "Your great IQ must be able to think of something better than, 'there, there.' I need help, Simon."

"All right," Simon said rubbing at his forehead like Aladdin at his lamp. "The old methods are probably the best."

"Name a few."

"Prayer, pilgrimage, a gift of sacrifice laid on the altar."

"I pray now," I said quickly. "I pray as well as I am able. I go about crying out, 'Oh, God. Oh, God,' and then I don't know quite what to say and I mumble."

"That's easily mended." Simon was soothing and unctuous as a flow of holy oil. "There are some printed rituals that will serve your purpose."

"But a pilgrimage . . ." I stopped bewildered. "Once around the island of Manhattan on the Circle Day Line? Through the United Nations on my lunch hour? What kind of a pilgrimage should I take?"

"One doesn't 'take' a pilgrimage," Simon said sternly, "one 'makes' a pilgrimage. One goes as far away from home as possible. One walks humbly and barefoot up the mountain and every step of the way one reflects on one's misdeeds."

I had had enough. I felt Simon was not taking me seriously and I was in no mood to be laughed at even if he thought all my sins were small and silly.

"Do you think I could be more miserable, Simon? Do you think anything worse than this could happen to me?"

"Yes," Simon said, "something much worse could happen to you." I had only said it out of pique because I was feeling sorry for myself but Simon had answered me with all the truth he had. I was wild with terror.

"Don't say any more, Simon. Be silent, do! I'll make a pilgrimage at once, barefoot, over jagged rocks and burning coals wearing a hair shirt dotted with prickly thorns, only don't say any more just now."

"All right," Simon said. He put his hands on my head, a sort of blessing and he said, "No more."

We never spoke of sacrifice. For if we had, I knew that the sacrifice would have to be a living one. It would have to be me.

THE ENTR'ACTE

17

I MADE quite a long pilgrimage, actually. I began it by going to England. They were doing a production of Jimmie
Dundee's play there. The British author wanted me to come
over and wear my hat. He felt it would bring them luck to
have me present. I said I would come at once. It was an
answer to my mumbled prayers to be able to get away so
easily.

Certainly Jimmie Dundee did not want to keep me from
going. Seeing each other every night at the theatre had
become a great strain for both of us. Jimmie Dundee was
laughably eager to let me go.

When I showed him the cablegram from England, he
snatched at it like the last straw on earth.

"You're sure you want to go?" Jimmie said, reading it over
and over.

"Absolutely sure," I said, watching his once-funny face now
so crumpled and worn.

"Then," Jimmie said, "I shan't stand in your way." And
he ran off quickly to count his blessings.

I sailed away on a ship of the Cunard Line. I went
Tourist Class. My cabin was below the sea and certainly
small and foul enough to satisfy the most flagellant of
monks. Simon came to see me off. He brought candy, books,
fruit, flowers and a week's supply of Dramamine.

"Don't you think," he said trying to find a place for everything, "that you are overdoing this hair shirt bit?"

"No," I said, "I'm giving the difference between First Class and this to the poor and I'm allowing myself the luxury of being anonymous. If I went First, I'd have to make conversation. Down here I can hide and rub salve on my wounds."

"All right then." Simon was obviously skeptical. "But do get up on deck for fresh air and drink a little lime juice every day. You don't want to fight scurvy as well as yourself."

"May I put rum in the lime juice?"

"As you choose," Simon said, "but don't forget to write."

"I'll write."

"Every day."

"Every single day."

Simon took me into his everlasting arms and held me there until the last gong was sounded for going ashore.

I began to write him before we left the territorial waters.

DEAR SIMON,

Have you ever heard of anyone being seasick while passing through the Narrows? I've mislaid the Dramamine and look forward to a lot of wretched retching.

DEAR SIMON,

I've been up on the little Tourist deck. They seem to empty the garbage from just below it which only makes me all the more homesick for you.

DEAR SIMON,

I've read all the mysteries of Agatha Christie. Is she not splendid? One can never remember a word, so can read them all over again instantly.

DEAR SIMON,

We are sure to sight land tomorrow. Will send you a faithful account of this pilgrim's progress. No doubt the world will burn all copies of *The Canterbury Tales* and put mine in their place.

DEAR SIMON,

Southampton today and the prospects of a boat train to Waterloo. Some fear and trepidation. I believe I'd rather get off at Elba and avoid the battle.

P.S. Have found Dramamine. Do Americans always arrive in England with too little too late?

DEAR SIMON,

I love London. I've thrown away the guide books and just wander. Everywhere I go, there is a familiar sight. I mean to say everything looks just like it does in the flicks. The Tower, St. Paul's, Piccadilly, Houses of Parliament, Buckingham Palace. The guards are impressive, so is the Abbey; when I am rich and virtuous, I'll buy Green Park. Then will you be my love? I'll build you a willow cabin at the gate and feed you on Dover Sole and Gulls' eggs.

All the people connected with the play seem very nice. They speak with British accents, which I find hysterical. I can't tell you just why. Do you know, the British need their umbrellas. They also need long underwear. I hope they have it. I've bought some. "Oh, to be in England now that April's here" is so much foolishness if one doesn't long for cold and drizzle.

We go to Manchester and to Leeds. They say Manchester is a jolly good audience but one can "die the death in Leeds." Can't understand what they are talking about half the time. They like my hat.

Simon, I miss you.

SIMON DEAR,

I haven't written because of the work. We stepped up the war effort and open in Manchester tomorrow night. Hotel in

Manchester, dreary! There's some law about not closing bathroom windows. The drafts are binding.

Simon, I'm going to call on my grandmother. Did you know I had one? Well, I do. Helen's mother lives here in Manchester. I wrote her a nice note and sent tickets for the opening. She wrote back, or rather a cousin did, to say grandmum couldn't make it because of her arthritis — but will I come to tea? I wrote back and said, yes.

Wish me luck for the opening.

DEAR SIMON,

The opening went well. The man playing Jimmie Dundee's part isn't as good as Jimmie but they like him. He's a big "Telly" favorite. Everyone else fine too. The comedy pace is much slower than in New York. I feared we might put them to sleep. Far from it! The audience was lively and wide awake. They laughed at all the jokes, including me. A funny hat's a funny hat, I always say.

Going to tea today at Grandmum's house — will tell all later.

Later: I don't know how to tell all. Absolutely ghastly covers it. Now to the particulars.

I had given the address written out on a slip of paper to the cab driver. When he pulled up in front of the house, he said most kindly, "Are you sure you can manage all right on your own, Miss?" I suppose he'd seen my face. That awful house, that awful street and those awful children standing about with their fingers up their dirty noses.

Dear old Helen. Don't know how she ever managed to get out, but my hat's off to her (no pun intended). No wonder she likes things grand and posh and genteel.

I didn't know Helen always sent home a little something to her dear old mum. I suppose now with the Labor government and socialized womb-to-tomb care, grandmum could manage without, but the pittance a week extra from Helen pays for the gin and Players.

The cousin who "looks after" grandmum is sponging off her but grandmum couldn't be let out alone. I only bring it up because if you think grandmum is a horror, you ought to see the cousin. Pure Hogarth.

There is a faded photograph on the mantel that seems to have been Helen's father. Grandmum kept talking about the late Mr. Shell in such a way as to make me fear his ashes, in an urn, might be forthcoming.

My, how the old thing does lap it up. Gin is indeed mother's milk to her. After she'd had quite a few drops taken, she slipped out of time sequence and got me confused with Helen. She went at me, or Helen, about being la-de-dah and putting on airs and fancying myself an h-actress. She kept asking why I wouldn't go into factory like a good girl and bring her home two pound ten a week instead of carrying on like I was h-Ellen Tarry. She grew quite abusive. Her basic English usage is extraordinary.

At blessed last, she passed out cold. The cousin said grandmum was easily tired and perhaps I'd better go, and I said, yes, perhaps I better had. The cousin said to come again if I could manage it and I said, yes, if I could manage it and I got out of there as fast as my lovely long-stemmed American beauty legs could carry me.

Two more things, just for the record. Two pounds ten is just what Helen sends her mum and the other thing is, cousin sold the tickets to the play so, in a way, I think the tea party was on me.

DEAR SIMON,

I now know what it means to "die the death" in Leeds. It means nobody likes you, nobody comes to the theatre. It means it rains so hard you start trying to book passage on the

Ark. It means you have the worst cold of your life and you're constipated beyond the help of Beecham's Pills.

Oh, Simon, Leeds is bloody awful!

DEAR SIMON,

The opening in London made up for Leeds. Fantastic and farfetched as that may seem in view of what I wrote you about Leeds, it's true. The press, penny and otherwise, has been smashing. They just couldn't have been nicer about everything and me especially. They say we're a new Crazy Gang. I'm crazy about being such a hit. Even though all that rattling of teacups and munching of chocolates at the interval tends to dismay this American actress who has never encountered anything more formidable than a whole audience full of bronchitis-stricken coughers.

Thank you for your opening-night cable. I got one from Helen, via Mr. Margolies, and one signed, Brandon and wife. The creature in the Western pants loves me at last. Oh, well, absence makes the heart grow fonder.

It does mine for you, at any rate. Are you working well? I'm to be on *What's My Line?* here.

DEAR SIMON,

As an alien, which I seem to be, I had to go round to some registration bureau and be queried. I'm not sure just why. Something to do with passport and work permit and other dull trifles.

Well, at the bureau, I met this little man, very civil-servant type. He was not actually wearing his bowler hat or carrying his bumbershoot, because he was at his desk when I met him, but he was so typically typical, I felt a great giggle coming on.

He harumphed and harumphed and ah-er looked at my papers and came to the conclusion I could ah-er stay in the ah-er country. Although I feel he secretly suspected me of being in the ill-paid employ of the IRA.

Then he got around to asking me if the ah-er Brandon Bradon listed on my ah-er papers was ah-er the Brandon Bradon who was the actor?

I said, yes, and before I could say, "Bob's your uncle," I had another relative or relation or whatever you want to ah-er call him.

He was most correct. Such a change from grandmum. He wished me ah-er every success and a pleasant stay in ah-er jolly old England. I said likewise I'm sure and offered to send him tickets for the play, which he ah-er accepted with pleasure. Although he harumphed, he ah-er said he must say he deeply regretted that Brandon, my ah-er father, had chosen the stage.

Why, I asked him, greatly surprised. Because, he ah-er said, Brandon was the first Bradon ever to leave the Civil Service.

Oh, Simon, I had to get out of his office before I laughed right in his ah-er face.

You know that was a most illuminating encounter. No wonder Brandon's always been a little dull and pompous. How could he help it with his background? Why, if Brandon hadn't won the beautiful face lottery, he'd be in some bureau ah-er harumphing away.

DEAR SIMON,

We've settled down to a routine run. I've gone out of an hotel into a service flat in Chelsea. Can't get enough of Mr. Whistler's bridges or the Thames. After I buy Green Park, I'm going to save up for the Royal Hospital and all the Chelsea Pensioners. Wasn't Nell Gwynn a living doll?

There's a chap in our play named Ronnie who has been taking me to the country to see the stately homes. He's not a new romance. He's not that sort but he's fun and he has an Aston-Martin.

We've been to Cambridge and to Oxford — Ronnie's old

school — he wears the tie. We've been to Windsor and to Warwick and to Blenheim.

Saw Stratford and Shakespeare at the source. Makes me feel so unlettered and untalented. What a playwright — what players.

Tea near Stratford.

And the lady who served up the tea was — have you guessed it? I suppose you're way ahead of me. Brandon's first wife.

Oh, Simon, she looks tired and pushed and as if she had been abandoned long ago. I had to say something to her but when I came right up to it, I didn't know what. So I asked her if there was a ladies' room and she said, yes. And I asked her if the weather was always so fine and she said no, and she went off to serve up some teas and I went to the loo and had a long think about how complicated and complex life can be.

I wish I had had the courage to ask her where Roland is.

DEAR SIMON,

I'm homesick. I want to come home. I've had it here. I've seen all the sights and all the sights have seen me. I feel as if I had been walking up the mountain for ever and ever. Isn't there supposed to be a shrine or a grotto or something to break up the monotony?

I think I'll go to Cornwall and sit on the edge of a Daphne du Maurier cliff and see if Iseult can't think of some way to get to Tristram even if he won't come to her.

Simon, are you really working so hard you can't get a jet and zoom on over?

DEAR SIMON,

You know what they say about the British penny press? Well, even if you don't, it's true. They are wild, libel-loving sharks — out for blood. Anybody's blood!

Usually they've got lots and lots of good eating in spies and call girls and Royal Family highjinks. Then just to dress up the pie, they throw in ax-murderers, poisoners, rapers, stranglers and ingenious dismemberers.

I tell you the truth, if I'd been brought up in England, I'd never speak to a strange man unless I first called in a policeman as witness. But not having been brought up here, I've been speaking to everybody in a nice, friendly American way. And as the law of averages would have it, I spoke to a gentleman of the press.

He got his Fleet Street wind up my family tree and in last Sunday's best paper there was a picture of me — in that hat — and a headline that asked, "Why won't Sir Edward Entertain His Son's Half-Sister?"

Sir Edward is Helen's cast-off chemist. He was terribly clever, chemically speaking, during the war and was rewarded with a knighthood. He also married his assistant in the lab who is now Lady Isobel. Just think, if Helen had hung on a bit longer, she could have been a lady and seen the Queen.

I had not, as you may imagine, contacted Sir Edward, nor had he seen fit to get in touch with me. I seriously doubt if he even knew I was here. But now, prodded by the press and perhaps by the fear of public ridicule and censure, there came an invitation to dine at his house.

I was in a state about what to wear. I changed three times, coming back at last to what I had had on at first. I rang up Sloane Square for a taxi and when it did not come, I rang for another. They both came at once and there were words.

Sir Edward lives in a tiny, perfect house off Wimpole Street — which struck me as ominous. There was a man to open the door and later a woman to wait at table.

But before the table, there were sherry and biscuits in the chill drawing room along with Sir Edward, Lady Isobel and the two half-brothers.

The half-brothers were shooting-stick straight and quite

correct. No angry young men they. Both are compensating conformists of great promise. One Cambridge; one Oxford. You see how eminently fair they are being. One Charles; one Philip. Such happy names for young Elizabethans. One is going for the Church, the other the Government. Both institutions might well beware their excess of zeal.

Sir Edward and Lady Isobel did not wear their white laboratory coats nor the half-brothers their college gowns. But they were all there to study me. I seemed at first glance better than they had bargained for and therefore all the more curious. How could I be Helen's daughter and presentable? It boggled their minds.

Not that anything unkind or painful was said. It was all done quite nicely. We managed a steady beat of conversation.

Did I like London? "Yes." Did I miss America? "Yes." Had I seen the Tower? "Yes." Hampton Court? "Yes." Madame Toussaud's? "Yes." Did I miss central heating? "Yes." Did I mind the damp? "Yes."

Sir Edward and Lady Isobel said they would like to visit America someday. One had met so many very civilized Americans during the war.

The half-brothers said they had heard America had the biggest and the newest, but surely I must agree England had the oldest and the finest.

We ate a pleasant dinner. Our jaws went up and down. We all looked each other in the face.

There was some of Helen in the boys. Just a fleeting expression, a set of the head now and again, and then it would vanish as soon as I saw it. If they have tried to exorcise Helen's spirit, they have succeeded. If Lady Isobel has not been a real mother to them, neither has Helen. They are self-sufficient, or at the worst, they have each other. Just as the two adorable babies of the new young wife in the Western pants have each other — and there in the middle of the muddle are the poor oaf Roland and me.

Sir Edward is certainly not Helen's style. He is Lady Isobel's style. She has not been above calling for bell, book and candle to rid her house of Helen.

They all have the same point of view about Helen. She has touched their lives just long enough to invest them with a disease of great discomfort. All the rest of their days, they will be obliged to have semiannual checkups just to be sure they have a clean bill of emotional health.

We said goodnight most graciously. They said they would come to the see the play. I said I would arrange tickets. They did not come. I did not expect them.

DEAR SIMON,

Never, never did I ever, ever expect to be in the movies but I'm going to be. I'm going to see Rome and get lots and lots of lovely lire to boot. Simon, I can't stop to write more now — I'm on my way to the airport.

DEAR SIMON,

I'm dying of frustration and despair. No wonder they pay people so much money to be in the moving pictures. They earn it seven times over.

When I got the offer to be in *The Last Days of Delilah* I was beside myself with pleasure. I spent good English pounds to buy myself out of the play in London. I must have been mad.

Full of beans and bliss, off I flew. Simon, I'm a prisoner in a Roman villa. I can't even find my way back to the airport. "They" picked me up in a limousine. All the way "here," I kept seeing a nightmare of lovely Italian landscapes befouled by indecent industrial structures.

"Here" is a villa within riding distance of Cinecitta. Every morning at five, "they" come and wake me up and drive me to the studio where "they" have built acres and acres of sets for *Delilah*.

But! You say to yourself, hasn't there been a recent film

about Samson and Delilah? You are quite correct. But this film takes place *after* Samson has pulled down the temple. In this film, Delilah has taken over the country and is sort of the Empress of sexual orgies. She can't get enough muscular young men to suit her. As soon as she seduces them, she has them thrown to the lions so they won't tell. (No, my dear, I don't know what she doesn't want them to tell.) The story outline was told to me by an Italian in a restaurant in Soho. There is no shooting script. "They" make it up as "they" go along.

Delilah is being played by the wife of one of the producers. She is terribly Italian and gorgeous. However, she has been at the pasta and has gotten so fat she can't be in any scenes until she boils off at least twenty pounds.

We have to shoot around her. I play her faithful handmaiden and I spend hours standing by her empty throne as thousands of dancing girls writhe and then just as the camera should turn upon Delilah and me the director yells "cut" in Italian.

I spend many more hours waiting to be summoned to pass a golden goblet to my queen who is not there. I spend many more hours waiting to look over a balcony and ask my nonexistent Empress if she does not indeed think those young men yonder are comely.

For all this, I am gotten up at five and by seven-thirty I'm in wig and gilt and long, flowing robes.

The star fat lady is locked up in her dressing room trailer. You can hear her crying out for food. When she becomes too restive and violent, "they" send in a masseuse who beats the tar out of her.

The leading man is an ex-wrestler from Newark, New Jersey. He is one big muscle. You might think this would make him perfect for the part. He has just one little problem. He can't retain his lines. One line at a time is his motto, which means "they" have to start and stop a good deal. He has a trainer who never leaves him for obvious reasons. The other day the trainer said to me, "Can you imagine this guy" — he pointed at his ward — "he's as great an actor as he is an athlete." I said, no, I couldn't imagine that.

Wish you could see me now. I've got on a headdress that squashes my brains, a cloak that weighs a ton, my nails have been pasted on, my eyelashes stick out to there, I've got on super wedges.

I'm supposed to be strumming on some yea old ancient Hebrew harp and there's nobody here but me.

This afternoon one of the lions (who are supposed to eat the seduced young men so they won't tell) broke loose. There was panic. I was not aware of the cause of the panic and chaos. It looked like an ordinary scene to me. I was sitting queenless in the royal barge waiting as usual when in jumped the lion. I really thought the pilgrimage had come to an end. But, no. The lion loved me on sight. I was quivering catnip. It rubbed up against me and purred like thunder. It breathed hotly in my face, its eyes slits of ecstasy. It had terrible halitosis. Finally, "they" came and caught it and reluctantly it was dragged away.

Simon, there has been a sign from heaven. "They" are suspending production. "They" have just found out that the fat lady star weighs more than she did when "they" put her on the diet. It's the masseuse that did it. She smuggled pasta into la star in her little black massaging bag.

The movies are not for me. I'm going to New York to read for a play. Leaving Rome tonight. What a pity to have been in the Eternal City and only seen Cinecitta.

DEAR SIMON,

I cannot believe the fates could have been so cruel. At the very moment I was landing in New York, you were landing in Rome. The very day I was in Cambridge to surprise you,

you were in Cinecitta to surprise me. (I'm glad you saw the set.) Now I'm off to read for that play in New York and you're on your way to Ethiopia and scroll land.

Simon, haven't I done enough penance? Is the pilgrimage not over? Let the comedy be ended.

THE HUMAN TRAGEDY

18

My wish came true. The comedy was ended. With the reading of the play the tragedy began. Mind you, I was the only one who seemed to feel it was a tragedy. Everyone else was quite gay and full of confidence. My agent believed it was going to be a triumph. I had called him the moment I had gotten back from Simonless Cambridge. I held the telephone with one hand and unpacked with the other.

"Hello," I said, "this is Diana."

"Diana baby, guess what?"

"What?"

"I've got you up for a lead."

"Bully for you."

"Can you guess the play?"

"No."

"Guess. Go on, guess."

"*Getting Gertie's Garter?*" My agent was aggrieved that I had missed the mark so wide. I became contrite. "I'm sorry," I said, "please tell me what's the play?"

"*Iphigenia in Aulis.*"

"You're kidding."

"No, why would I kid you, baby?"

"What part?"

"Why Iphigenia, the lead, of course. Every girl in New York wants the part."

I didn't want to hurt his feelings but it did occur to me that he had gone right out of his flesh-peddling mind. I knew nothing about being a classic heroine. I'd had trouble enough being a teen-age girl friend or a girl in a hat or the handmaiden who was not there.

"Look," I said cautiously, tentatively, "do you think Greek tragedy is quite my style?"

"Sure," said my agent. He was always so positive in his ignorance. "Now you gotta see them tomorrow at three-thirty at the Booth Theatre. Do you think you can make that?"

"I think so."

"Good girl," he said, and "lotsa luck." He hung up.

I hung up and finished unpacking. I discovered I had left my umbrella in Rome. It did seem an evil omen and I was full of anxiety. No Simon, no umbrella, no mother to guide me. I had a sudden gigantic presentiment that I was to be staked out naked before the world totally exposed and absolutely defenseless.

I pulled myself together and went to see "them" the next afternoon at three-thirty. My agent was right about every girl in New York wanting the part. Shubert Alley was packed, jammed from the sidewalks of Forty-fifth Street to the sidewalks of Forty-fourth Street with wanting girls.

Fat, tall, thin, short, blonde, brunette, redheaded and in-between girls. Some with, some without agents, mothers or friends of their bosoms and all eager as could be to speak the speeches of tragedy. An assistant stage manager checked off my name from a long list on his clipboard. He gave me a mimeographed speech to look over. I did not understand a word of it. I waited, stifling in a garden of female flowers.

Then I was summoned. My name called out before others who had been waiting far longer. The flowers looked at me like inmates at Belsen looking at the one who has escaped the gas chamber. I left them to their fate, and went into the theatre.

The "Them" I was supposed to see were three producers called the Producers' Group. They were all young, wore gray flannel suits and large, black-rimmed glasses. Some wag had said that they were all one and the same, for one rarely saw them together. They were producing this play in association with the Partridge Foundation Committee for the American Theatre. Some wag had said that the Partridge Foundation was giving away its money alphabetically and had just this year come to the letter T.

This version of Euripides' play had been translated into a very blank verse by an Iowa poet who had never gotten any closer to Aulis than Cedar Rapids. No wag said anything about him. WHAT COULD ONE SAY? He was so limited of vision that he had reduced the high rock of tragedy to the dimension of a homecoming game with Notre Dame.

The production was being conceived and staged by Sir Arthur St. Alyot, who had staged a coronation and as a result believed in typecasting. It was his boast that he could take whores from brothels, chimney sweeps from chimneys, plumbers from sewers and make actors of them if only they were the right type.

As I stumbled from the sun-blinding alley into the bat-dark cave of the theatre I could not see any of their faces but I heard them out front whispering and tittering, keeping each other company in the dark house. I was alone on the stage with one ghastly work light and a frenzied stage manager who had forgotten that the only object of the day was to choose an actress to play Iphigenia and who had come to believe that his true task was to get as many girls on and off the damp, dark stage in as short a time as humanly possible. He was surely a figure of Greek tragedy, a sort of Sisyphus of Shubert Alley. Every time he rolled in an actress there was another one at the door, a bigger and bolder one than before; crushing, bearing down on him, driving him fair mad.

"Read, read," he snarled, "we haven't got all day."

I was suddenly enraged. My rage was infantile and uncontrolled. I was a baby who had discovered that the world was a comfortless and careless place. My face contorted, my feet stamped. I roared and cried into the dark void.

"What do you mean read, read, you haven't got all day? This whole affair is lunatic. I was supposed to come at three-thirty. I have been waiting well over an hour standing like cattle in that silly alley. I have been given a paragraph to speak which is totally meaningless out of context. I might as well have gotten it out of the weighing machine at Woolworth's. You don't dare to show your faces and I'm supposed to expose my whole being by one dirty electric light bulb. Well, thank you kindly one and all, but no thank you." I balled up the paragraph and threw it at the stage manager's feet. I ran from the theatre down the alley across Broadway and over to Schrafft's where I had a caloric coffee soda and thought of what I should have said to them but had not and then I went to a marathon Biblical movie, after which technicolor entertainment there was nowhere to go but home.

When I got back to by sublet I found the messengers of the gods had been working overtime. There were messages from just everyone. They all wanted me to know how sorry they were to have caused me inconvenience or distress. The producers three, the Partridge Foundation, the corny poet, the manic and egotistical director, the stage manager and the light bulb. They all wanted me to please, please come and read again. The phone rang, it was my agent. He said, "I hear you were great, just great. They all want you to read again."

My presentiment of desolation began to grow cold and rumble like the loosening rock of an avalanche. What was so

appallingly, unutterably awful to me was not that they had
eaten humble pie but that I knew I was going to get the part.
I was going to be chosen for living sacrifice.

I went to see them a second time. They were very nice. I
was very nice. We all shook hands. They heard me read.
Then they heard me read again. We all shook hands again.
They said they were looking for a type, a quality, and that
they were going to see other girls and did I understand and
was that all right? I said of course I understood and please to
go right ahead and read anyone they thought might do. But I
knew they were going to choose me. The more they rolled
their eyes and licked their lips and said, would you mind
most dreadfully if we asked you to read again, would it be
too off-putting if we asked you to come and see us just once
more, the more I said, no, it mattered not at all to me. I was
tranquilly chewing on the betel nut of negation. I was
passive, inhaling the gases of the oracles preparing for the
sure and lethal end of my being.

Meanwhile hysteria in the female theatrical community
grew to an alarming pitch. A society never known for its calm
approach to even the simplest problems was not confronted
with a true test of its strength and endurance. There was
much weeping and wailing and gnashing of teeth. Lamps
went out, there was no more oil. Some were taken to
Bellevue, some took to pills, some took to the river. It was
horrid and silly and a terrible waste because the die had been
cast in my lap. At last "They" announced that the part was
mine. The news was officially printed in the *New York
Times*. My agent was exultant and exhausted. He called,
gasping with fatigue.

"Well," he said, "you got the part, what do you think of
that?"

"Oh," I said, "I think it's going to end in tears. I do, I
really do."

19

IF it did not end in tears it was sure to end in madness. I
had never seen a rehearsal as disorganized. No rented hall
for tragedy, no parquet floors or clouded mirrors, no summer
loft sweet with the scent of remembered hay. For tragedy
we rehearsed on a tennis court under the blazing sun. I lay
stretched out on the top of a pile of packing crates pretending I was lying on a rock at Aulis. I wished I had been at
Aulis or anywhere but here. The director, Sir Arthur St. Alyot,
sat above the tennis court in the referee's chair commanding
us from above like an Assyrian king from a golden chariot.
He spoke into a megaphone, his words echoed and rever-
berated like doom in white flannels.

"Surge in," he bellowed. In surged the chorus."No, no,
no," he groaned, "surge in swiftly, speak and surge out."

It was ridiculous. I had to laugh. I lay broiling and
laughing, the tears pouring down my cheeks. At least they
were cool to my parched skin.

We were not rehearsing in the city because the weather
had gone haywire. It was the hottest September in the
memory of man or the history of the weather bureau. Air
conditioners had worked beyond their capacity and had
failed. The city was in a blackout. Policemen turned their
Nelson eyes to children bathing in the waters of fire hydrants
in the light of the silvery moon. By day the city streets

reflected the orange ball of fire in the heavens. Old crones muttered imprecations of disaster in deserted A & P's, their faces blank as ancient priestesses, their hairy chins trembling with the fear of what they foretold.

Our company was the elite. We were the pets of the privileged. We were removed by chartered bus to a Long Island estate once the home of, now the Foundation of, Partridges. There we were billeted in the great house. We were wined and dined in the long hall, we were rehearsed privately like royal players on the tennis court, commanded by imperative St. Alyot and observed from the bleachers by the producers three, the playwright, the scene designer, the costume designer and their assistants, the actors not in the rehearsing scene and assorted Partridge-type employees, these grooms and knights of the garters and grounds.

They all seemed to think we were an amusing sight, more amusing than dancing bears or trained dogs or marionettes on strings. Every morning at a given signal we hopped up on our marks and began to perform our tricks.

We were most certainly a mixed bag of strolling players.

America's own Blanche Prichette Ives had been coaxed out of retirement to play Clytemnestra, which translated meant she had not been working lately and was beside herself with joy at the thought of appearing before the public.

Wilhelm Bentz Plagemann had been imported from the West German State Theatre to play Agamemnon, which meant he had at last been cleared of all Nazi activities and allowed to enter the country.

Douglass Horvak, a former Mr. Atlas, had been engaged to play Achilles. He often did not understand what he was saying and would pause to flex a muscle while he mulled it over.

There was Actors' Equity's oldest member to play the senile high priest who assisted at the sacrifice. I hoped he'd find the knife and the stage on the same night. There was a fashion model to play the goddess Diana. She had mislaid a false fingernail our first day in the country and talked of her loss constantly. There were assorted alarms, excursions, messengers from without as well as a chorus of maidens who all looked like bridesmaids at a fashionable garden wedding.

I thought the new version of the play was dreadful but I was alone in that opinion. Everyone else loved it. It was said by all that it had great stature and reached new heights.

The playwright loved it most of all. He sat in the stands like a bird on a perch mouthing every word. He held the script in his lap fancying himself Shakespeare at the Globe, the first folio in his grasp. What had been a tragedy of characters whose flaws and cracks had appeared fully revealed in the light of Aulis had become in this playwright's hands, a country-club crise.

That other Agamemnon, who had been willing to expiate his guilt by the sacrifice of his own child's flesh so that a wind would blow for his comrades and the fleets of war, became now only an all-American businessman eager to be off on a commercial venture.

That other Clytemnestra who had royal hate and vengeance sweet on her lips was here only an ambitious matron seeking status in an advantageous marriage for her daughter. Achilles was merely a popular favorite, a man of the moment with no destiny to fulfill.

Iphigenia was gormless to an idiotic degree, willing to go anywhere she was bidden as long as she could leave home. She was suddenly in a state of shock to find herself the victim of the month there on that high rock, the reality of the dagger above, caught at last as resourceless as a high-school cheerleader faced with middle age.

Yet everybody loved it but me. The Partridge Foundation for American Arts had chosen an American architect to build them an indoor amphitheatre in the neo-Grecian style in New York City. We were to be honored to open the new theatre. Well, if the Partridge Foundation wanted seventeen Corinthian columns they were in a position to pay for them.

Through the weeks of that hot September we rehearsed on the acres of the tax-exempt and made Corinthian and Doric and Ionic attitudes of our shadows.

"You're going to be a star," Blanche Prichette Ives said to me. "You're going to be a star, my dear."

Sir Arthur kissed my hand.

"Oh boy, you're going to be a star all right," said the playwright. That was nice to hear but how could they tell? Was it from the way I lay stretched out on a cascade of boxes? Was it the degree of my sunburn? I was burned beyond the repair of any bleach cream. I was a broiled lobster, the meat detaching from my bones. I sought what protection I could find under a large beach hat which was not quite large enough to cover all of me at any one time. I did not feel like a star, I prayed for a saviour, someone, something, anything to take away my pain of isolation. I wished I could be turned into one of Diana's deer and whisked away to Tauris to serve forever in the sacred grove. It would be a positive pleasure to spend out my life guarding her image while entertaining all those fascinating tortured souls who dropped in to beg favors of the deity.

"In Germany you would already be a star," said Wilhelm Bentz Plagemann.

"You're going to be a star," said the producers three in chorus. They did look exactly alike.

"You're going to be a star," said the press agent, and "How's your mother? Could we have some pictures of the two of you together? Helen Shell's daughter to be star, that sort of thing."

"No," I said, "no pictures."

I had not seen Helen since I got back from England but Mr. Margolies said she was no better, no worse.

"You're going to be a star," said the costume designer as he draped my royal Grecian robes.

"Is this what I'm wearing?" I demanded, hot and out of patience.

"Yes," he simpered. "I can always tell a star."

"It's a bedsheet," I said accusingly.

"How clever of you to guess." His lips compressed.

"Not at all, it looks like a bedsheet."

"Well, you're not a real star yet, you know. You must wait till you are a real star to bitch about the costumes. So there!"

20

WHEN we left the country and moved the show into the ersatz temple of Thespis all the costumes looked like bedsheets, all the scenery like abandoned orange crates. The lights fell into pools so small one could not see the players who stood in between. The playwright would not cut or re-write a line and still everyone said it was going to be a tri-umph. My agent came to a preview at which exhibit the piano wire that was supposed to fly me out of the way of all mortal harm got tangled and I was left dangling in midair as the curtain came down.

"Oh baby, oh doll," my agent said, "it's going to be une magnifique, un triomphe!"

Well, maybe it was just me. I must be wrong. It must be that I hadn't yet got the hang of blank verse. Surely just at the last minute, just in time's nick I would get the message from the gods. Someday soon I would understand the words and see the actors' faces and a performance starlike to at least a dim degree would emerge for public view.

At the moment I did not understand one word I said. I did not see anything but blurs and shadowy shapes. I was detached and estranged from the play and the players. I was out of touch with the preview audience. There was not one shred of reality in any moment of the entire production. I was as frightened as a silent-picture star in a talking-picture world.

I cabled Simon a little pleading cable. Ethiopia was very far away and an airmail letter seemed too unreliable.

SIMON

Help I'm being held prisoner in a Greek tragedy. I don't want to be Iphigenia at Aulis or anywhere else. Save me, save me. Au secours as my agent would say.

Simon cabled back.

DIANA

Forget Greece, Ethiopia is the place. Did you know that the ancient world believed the gods came to Ethiopia to dine? They believed that the sun set here. So do I. I believe the sun rises and sets in this place. Once a year the rains come and wash it all away to Egypt but there's still a lot left at least for the moment. I must work quickly, they are talking of building a dam across the valley and if they do it will flood the caves. It is my last chance to discover something of value. I'm off to dine with the gods on a tin of Spam.

As always,

SIMON

I did not know what to do. In a foolish panic I went to see Helen. I stole the day from the Aulis company. I was supposed to be at the wigmakers but with all the heads to camouflage I thought they would not miss mine.

Helen was in the billiard room at the Abide Awhile Rest Home. She was working on a gigantic jigsaw puzzle. She was assembling it on the billiard table. She was looking very well, I thought. She wore her glasses without being self-conscious. She was absorbed in her work. She looked older but better in a country lady sort of way. She was wearing a brown tweed skirt and sweater set with a single strand of pearls.

"Nice of you to come," she said without looking up. I gave

her a small hug and a tiny kiss. She did not stiffen or pull away but neither did she lean in toward me.

"How are you, Helen?" I asked for want of something better.

"I'm just fine, thank you," she said as though she always was. "I'm looking for a piece with blue at the edge and maybe a dot or two of red. Be a dear and see if you can see it."

I looked about and found a piece I thought might do. I handed it to her.

"No," Helen sighed, "that's not it, I've already tried it and it doesn't fit."

"What's it going to be when you finish?"

"I don't know," Helen said brightly. "That's the challenge. It makes it much harder, don't you think?"

"Yes, I do," I agreed sincerely.

Helen rummaged on trying to find a blue-edged piece with red dots to fill the gap.

"I've been to England and come home again," I said.

"Have you, dear?" Helen tried another shape and found it wanting. "Did you see the Queen?" she asked slyly.

I was peeved at the old nursery approach. I wanted to blurt out, "I didn't see the Queen but I saw your mum."

"Well, yes actually," I said, "I did see the Queen at a command film performance. Then I went from England to Rome and now I'm home. Everyone was very kind," I said lamely.

"Too bad." Helen shook her head; I thought she had meant the puzzle but she continued, "Really too bad that I don't have any family left in England for you to see." Helen sighed again. "What a pity you never got to know my mum."

I didn't know what to say to Helen. Was she mad or sane?

Helen went on, oblivious, "If only my mother had been living what a time you could have had with her."

"What?" I gasped, incredulous.

"There," Helen cried in triumph. She had found the piece she had been searching for. "Now, dear," she became very confidential, "if you could look for a sort of pinkish squiggly bit." I looked blindly in the maze.

"You never told me your mother was dead," I mumbled.

"Oh, yes, dead," Helen said and gave me her tragic gaze, "surely I told you."

"No, you did not tell me."

"Oh, yes, I did. You've just forgotten. It was years ago. You were only a baby. She died in her sleep. I only hope I go that way."

"You never told me."

"Yes, dear." Helen's tone was sharp indeed. "I did. You just weren't paying attention. She was a most remarkable woman. She sacrificed herself for me. Never thought of herself . . . always of others. Sad you never knew her, you would have loved her. You're very like her."

"I am?" I was flabbergasted.

"Yes," Helen purred, "in some ways very like." I did not know for the life of me whether Helen believed what she was saying or whether she was having me on for her afternoon joke.

"Mother was a lady," Helen said firmly, "a great lady. She married beneath her and was disinherited but she never complained. She was a wonder." Helen's eyes misted with tears. I felt I must change the subject.

"Listen, Helen," I said, "I'm in a new play."

"Are you?" Helen wiped away a tear. "That's nice, what sort of hat do you wear in this one."

"I don't wear a hat," I said, "I wear a bedsheet." That caught her attention.

"You're pulling my leg."

"Afraid not, Helen. It's a bedsheet all right. I'm in a classical tragedy."

"You?" Helen turned to me incredulous. "You can't be serious. You in a classic?"

"I'm dead serious. I'm Iphigenia at Aulis."

"My God." Helen rolled her eyes and began to laugh.

"Yes," I said, "I know I'm out of depth. I'm not up to it. I hate the play. I hate me in it."

"When do you open?" Helen grew serious.

"Next week."

"Well, this is no time to say you are bad."

"I didn't say I was bad," I bristled, "you said that. I said I didn't think I was quite up to it. I hate it. I don't like the stage any more. It's hateful and loathsome."

"Oh, that." Helen relaxed her gaze. "Of course you hate it, my dear, the stage is a loathsome place."

"You don't understand me," I wailed, "why won't you ever try to understand me?"

"Self-pity," Helen snorted, "will get you in the nuthatch just like me." I assumed an attitude of wounded dignity.

"You don't know what I'm going through."

"You just think I don't know what you're going through. I bloody well do. You'll get over it."

"I won't get over it." I was in a fury.

"What does it matter that you loathe the stage all of a sudden? You still have to open, so why come sniffling to me that you hate your job. Everybody hates their job, that's life."

"I hate life then."

"Of course you do." Helen was clearly bored. "But if you are going to come all this way to visit me then you might at least try to keep your problems to yourself, and make yourself useful. I'm supposed to be ill and hospitals are Kings X."

"All right, Helen, I'm sorry." I saw it was no use. "How can I be helpful?"

"By looking for the pinkish squiggly bit." I looked but I

did not find it. Even when it got to be teatime and I had to go I tried to reach out once more.

"I've tried to help you with your puzzle," I said, "haven't you any help for me?" I was truculent. "Any little words of wisdom would be appreciated."

"Yes, I have a word for you," Helen said owlishly. "Just remember that eleven o'clock will come."

I turned on my heel and ran away.

21

E LEVEN o'clock did come. Clutching Helen's nugget of theatrical wisdom to my percale-covered bosom, I waited for the curtain to go up on opening night. It was an auspicious occasion. One could tell because Brandon and Helen both sent telegrams, Mr. Margolies orchids, Simon sent an Ethiopian artifact of utility or fertility — I could not tell which. The Partridge Foundation sent a horseshoe of roses as if I had already won the Derby without running the race. The whole evening was a little hind-part-beforehand, a little déjà vu.

Most of the kissing went on before the curtain went up, not after it came down. The producers three kissed me on each cheek, that's six kisses from them, the playwright kissed me and maddened me with his remark, "How nice to have you in my beautiful play." What brass! It wasn't even his plot. The costume designer kissed me and gave me a frosty smile as he adjusted my robes de mariage. Sir Arthur St. Alyot roamed the halls kissing everybody and reading his telegrams from royalty aloud, calling out their names like stations on the Brighton line.

This evening might be a funeral, but if it was it was the funeral of a very old and distant uncle whose timely demise had left one independently wealthy. The cast pretended to jitters they did not have. The Partridge Foundation did not have flops. The worst thing that ever happened to them was a succès d'estime, or at rock bottom a worthwhile artistic experiment long needed on the theatrical scene.

For me there was still a tiny hope that there might be some magic and some glitter, that when the curtain went up I would be transformed into another self, that the white bedsheets would be transformed into the wedding robes of Iphigenia, that a wind would blow across the rocks at Aulis and that the goddess would transform a poor, helpless creature into a sacred deer and take her away to a divine and sacred grove. I prayed for armies of the redheaded brother to sail across the wine-dark sea. I prayed for Clytemnestra to sink into the arms of Aegisthus to plot a ten-year scheme of revenge. I prayed that I might not be hung up dead on strands of piano wire without any hope of pretending otherwise.

The curtain went up, the chorus moaned and groaned. All hope went up with the curtain, vanished up the spouts of artificial light. There was no miracle. I saw everything through my own eyes and I saw nothing but actors in silly sheets. I saw naked knees, I saw wigs made of human hair glued onto human skulls with strips of netting colored over with Stein's greasepaint. I saw broken veins and sweating armpits. I saw expensive dentures and padded bosoms. I saw nothing but reality. There was no transformation nor none coming forever more.

I could have cried out, O ta ta toi, with the chorus and sat on the ground and covered up my head so that my eyes might not see and my ears might not hear the senseless drama going on around me. Instead I said my lines by rote and said all the speeches given to me by the bard of Iowa. I pronounced them as trippingly from my tongue as if they had been Shakespeare's best. On and on I spoke as I was spoken to until at last in the final moment of the play I lay stretched out on a great painted papier-mâché rock,

Agamemnon above me, knife in hand. He raised it high, glittering and shining in the bastard amber light. I sighed in relief. It was a welcome sight, that knife, it was a cue that the end of the play was nearly over.

I had Helen's philosophy to cling to. Eleven o'clock was on its way. There was no real danger here, only the contorted visage of Wilhelm Bentz Plagemann, full of sound and fury, meaning nothing. He was no real Nazi, only a draper's dummy, a decoy for the unwary. I suddenly remembered a cartoon of a baby standing alone with a blanket for company clutched to its side and the caption that read, "I don't want to be a victim, I want to be a winner." As the knife came down toward me the deus ex machina appeared. I felt the tug of the fly-away wires and I was hoisted to heaven. I broke into laughter. I howled with the comedy of life tickling my ribs. I disappeared into the wings, the trapdoor beneath the papier-mâché rock opened, and there where I had been lying but a moment before was a stuffed deer. Oh, what magic for the audience and what a giggle for me to see its two blind glass eyes.

The curtain fell, stagehands unleashed me from my fly-harness and I went on for the curtain call. The applause was a roar from the faraway sea. Wilhelm Bentz Plagemann squeezed my hand and whispered, "Liebchen, you became a star in that last scene. I have never beheld such emotion, so true, so real. You will remember this night forever."

22

INDEED I did remember that night forever. Not because I became a star but because it was the night I met my someone to love and my someone to love me. I was ready for him to appear. Until the curtain rang down on Iphigenia I had no idea how much I wanted to be the winner of the lucky love lottery and not the victim of the games and festivals, or how little chance I thought I had of that really happening to me. There, suddenly in my mind was an end to playing dress-up. The fun and the games were ended. The salt had lost its savor. The luster was lacking. I could perform no more feats of magic in the enchanted wood. I could no longer hide in the identity of the parts I played. I had to be me. Unfortunately I did not know who I was. What made this night different from all other nights was that I became convicted of the notion that I had passed through the seven tortures and tests and that now I was entitled to the prize in the box of Cracker Jacks and the prize is always love.

The opening-night party given by the Partridge Foundation was one big box of Cracker Jacks. I had never seen anything like it. No Sardi's for the Partridge Foundation, no public restaurant. The Partridge Foundation did things properly. The Partridge Foundation hired a ballroom with rose-brocaded walls. They summoned a chef from France, imported the vintage wines of the world. They engaged a string quartet to sit out of sight and play discreet evocative tunes.

The acting company had been instructed to dress and stand in a receiving line to meet the great and the near-great and the grayly eminent. I stood between Agamemnon and Clytemnestra looking like sacrificial lamb dressed up as cultural mutton. It was my debut to meet the world. My coming-out party given at great danger and expense to the management. I was compelled to stand and receive what homage there was coming to me. Not a sincere word was uttered. It was a second show without a script. It became a commedia dell'arte of dilettantes. Decorations blazed past, a tiara curtseyed before me.

"You were wonderful, my dear."

"Simply marvelous. So lovely."

"So radiant, my dear."

"What a performance, my dear." We all looked like dress extras propped up before the potted palms, a charade of royal highjinks in a kingdom as foolish and spurious as Ruritania.

I searched my mind for a suitable pose and decided on humility as being what was wanted. I smiled demurely and dropped my eyes and managed a blush for my cheeks. It was the silliest and most insincere night of my entire theatrical life.

When I had shaken the last hand I was given meat and drink; champagne for fun and caviar for frolic. All the Iphigenia company was seated at one big round table so they might be studied as an ethnic group by their assembled betters. The players and their kind are always fascinating to the barons of society. They feel they must encourage the poets and the players and the minstrels but they would not necessarily want to eat with them.

I did not mind being a creature in their zoo. They had gone to a great deal of trouble to gather us together to watch us at our feeding time and they had provided us with excellent victuals.

Another night I would have been in a rage to be so exposed but this different night I knew I was going to escape. I was going to make a mighty leap and go out over the walls of my ingeniously constructed enclosure. So let them look and gaze to the end of their curiosity. By tomorrow I would have changed my spots and stripes and taken on the protective coloring of an ordinary human being in the real world.

At last at midnight there came a fanfare. The early papers, *Times* and *Tribune*, were brought on a silver salver to St. Alyot, who reigned over us at the big round table. He read aloud in a full, fine voice. Such hubris I shall never see again. He had no fear the news would be a disgrace. The gods had already been propitiated by the kings of the earth. I heard my name called out by St. Alyot. I was considered luminous and lovely and lyrical. I was not a star but I was a member of the community in better than good standing.

What did it matter to me tonight that my news was good news? The slipper had fallen from my foot, the golden coach had turned into a pumpkin, my finery was all rags and tatters, the ball was over. I sat by an unswept hearth, the world tasted of ashes in my mouth. I wanted to go home but I had no home to go to. I did not even have an umbrella to call my own. I wanted to cry. I felt so sorry for me. I was wild to get out of that hateful room.

I looked about for the nearest exit, a little door to creep through unnoticed, and as I cast about for a way out of my predicament I saw this marvelous gingerbread boy standing by a potted palm looking at me with adoring raisin eyes. He was so beautiful, so pink and brown I had to have him for my own. He was totally edible. I wanted to eat him instantly. I smiled at him. He leapt in my direction as eager as a brandy-logged Saint Bernard.

"Is there anything I can do for you?" he asked.

146

"Yes," I said, "you can take me away from all this."

He got me out of there with great authority and dispatch. He was superbly masterful with coat checks and the elevator. He was supremely in control of finding a taxi. He told the cabbie to drive around Central Park. We talked and talked and drove and drove around and around.

His name was Stanley Partridge, the Third. He was very quick to add that he was not one of the rich Partridges. He said he was a very poor Partridge indeed, but he had the name so they let him play the game. They had found him a place in the scheme of things working for the Partridge Foundation. He was a junior expert on depressed areas and reclamation projects. I laughed and he wanted to know why and I said: "I think I may be the most depressed area you have ever encountered. I think I may be your finest hour in reclamations." But I saw that he did not understand what in the world I meant and I was not sure I could explain it to him just yet.

He was so pleased to be going around Central Park in a cab with me. Whenever we completed a full-lap circle he would lean forward and say to the driver, "Just once more, please." He still could not believe his fortune that I had smiled at him. Well, I insisted I did. I was very adamant about it. I said, "I smiled at you, Stanley."

"But why me, of all people?" I hadn't the heart to tell him it was because he was there when I needed him.

"I think," I said, "it's because you made me think of the gingerbread man who ran and ran as fast as he could away from the little old lady and the little old man and never, never let anyone eat him up, not even the fox."

"Isn't that odd," said Stanley, furrowing his brow. "I thought the fox ate him."

"No," I said in a panic, "no one ate the gingerbread man, and I'm not a fox, I'm not, I'm not."

147

"Of course you're not," Stanley smiled, contented in his ignorance of his danger. "You're a star."

"No, I'm not a star, I'm only a proficient player and I'm not going to be that much longer. You'll see."

"A star," he insisted. He made the cabdriver take us to Times Square to buy the morning papers and then we drove back into the park again. Stanley switched on the overhead light and read me the tabloid notices. They were very good. Better than the *Trib* or the *Times* for me. They liked the look of me and the sound of me. They thought I was a pretty girl in a bedsheet and they admired me for it.

Stanley thought I was a pretty girl too. He was admiring and gazing and breathing heavily. Surely he knew that if he played his cards right he could kiss me there in the taxicab.

But he did not, would not. I did not know why but he insisted on taking me home at once so I could get my rest. He said it was because I had to be fresh for the theatre. Well, it wasn't what I wanted but I had to settle for that and the news that he would pick me up after the play and take me out to supper.

How Stanley loved being my stage-door Johnnie. How proud he was to wear me on his arm when we went into a restaurant. I chose Sardi's because I knew he would like for me to be recognized and made over. It didn't hurt me and it gave him a monumental gift of pleasure.

We had gotten to the coffee before all the table-hoppers had hopped at me, chirped their nonsense and hopped away again. Stanley grew quiet and introspective; he began to chew at his lip.

"What is it?" I asked. I couldn't stop myself. I knew it was unwise. If you want a true answer you must never ask a true question.

"There is something I think you ought to know," he said. I saw that he had to tell me something that he did not want to tell at all. It was his little true confession time.

Oh, dear, I thought, he's already married to a girl in Outer Liberia and has seven children under the age of eight. But it was nothing like that. He wanted to tell me about his father. His father had been a proper rich Partridge but Stanley Partridge II had been a very bad bird indeed. He had fiddled the family fortune down the drain and then had flown the coop leaving behind him Stanley and his mother. His mother, Stanley said, had given up her life for him. She had even gotten him his job with the Partridge Foundation.

Dear, sweet Stanley to feel he must lay the blot on his scutcheon out before me so that I could accept or reject his piece of damaging news. It made me feel very sentimental and soft toward him.

"Tell me more about your father," I said.

"We never mention him," Stanley looked grieved.

"Oh, dear," I said, "only one perfidious parent. I have two, you see," I said as gently as I could but it startled him quite a good deal.

"How's that?" he blurted.

"Brandon and Helen," I said. "Mummy and Daddy — they were both bolters and abandoners of the worst sort. Not totally perfidious, you understand, but gone — you know, not there — not ever. I'm very insecure, very dependent."

"My mother is splendid," Stanley said, "really fine. How she has managed I don't know. It's been very hard for her to bring me up alone. You can see that can't you?"

"Yes," I said, "I can. I'm sure that she's a brave, little woman."

"Oh, she is," Stanley said, "she is." I loved Stanley, he was so dear, so serious, so sincere.

I began to see a lot of Stanley. I saw him every night. He liked calling for me and I liked knowing he would be there when the curtain came down. It made the last part of that dreadful play so much more bearable. I did not mind Agamemnon standing above me with the knife or the phony

149

goddess or the pull of the piano wire if I knew in a few minutes there would be Stanley waiting and adoring me for being a star in great danger and peril of her life.

I knew Stanley would save me. I made up my mind to marry him as soon as he could convince himself that he was worthy of me. Courtship was obviously a ritual to Stanley without which no romance could be possible. We had to proceed in an acceptable social fashion. So while we were going from dinners to long drives in the country to the meeting of his mother I began to plan my trousseau and to buy some pretty linens for my hope chest.

It was Christmas before he could even get himself to take me home to meet his mum. She lived in Tarrytown on the remains of a Partridge estate. She lived in the hunting lodge which had been her dower portion at the time of the divorce. She was very brave and did good works and sat on committees and wore sensible tweeds and suitable crepe frocks and pigged along on the unearned income of her divorce settlement. She had been reduced to this humiliating poverty by the perfidious conduct of the long-gone father.

She did her best to make me feel welcome. She had shined the diamonds and cleaned the pearls. She was quick to say she loved the theatre and wished as a girl that she had been allowed a career on the stage. She had seen Helen and Brandon in their war play and she had admired them mightily. She said if Stanley were ever to marry she would be pleased to have him choose a wife from the stage. But she lied. She knew she lied and I knew that she lied and she knew that I knew that she lied.

She served us tea. We trimmed the tree and had escalloped oysters and champagne and went to Christmas Mass. We opened our presents early Christmas morning and all had a jolly time roasting the goose and pouring the brandy on the plum pudding. Stanley lit it with a flourish and carried it flaming to the head of the table. The servants had been given the day off and we were just the family to serve ourselves. Stanley sat at the head of the table, a small master in his mother's house.

Later we had tea again and then we drove back to the city so that I could make my evening performance on time. We rode into town bundled in our winter overcoats, the car heater blowing the breath of hell on our legs. Stanley began to perspire. It was more than our enclosed confinement to each other; it was a sheer panic of nerves. I did not sweat but my mouth was as dry as the Gobi.

"Well," said Stanley at last, "what do you think?"

"I think," I said walking on eggshells and broken Steuben glass, "that your mother is very beautiful and very brave." Stanley sighed in relief and began to whistle a merry Christmas tune.

Still, it was spring before he could bring himself to pop the question. In the early spring he began to feel the sap running in his veins, and unable to deny that he felt an overpowering physical urge to make mad passionate love to me, he asked me to marry him; marrying and mating being synonymous in his code book.

"Will you marry me?" he asked, stricken with courage.

"Yes," I said at once, "I think we must lock big toes and limp through life together." My haste to say yes frightened Stanley so that he insisted that we not have the ceremony until my play closed. He said it would not be fair to me, he did not want to cheat me out of my career. I agreed to his decision. I was in a mood to humor him.

"I love you, Stanley," I said.

"I love you," he said, "but what do you see in me?"

From that day forward every day until the day we were married, every single day he said, "I love you, but what do you see in me?" and I said:

"I love you, what do you see in me?"

23

NEITHER of us seemed to have an answer to the question, so we went on asking it in a pleasant, rather mindless fashion while we kissed and fondled, which was more mindless and more pleasant. Time rushed on toward a wedding day, that wonderful day when the play would close and the final curtain would fall. It was a dream of life, it was warm and moist like the rains of heaven falling on the first planted seeds; nothing sprouting, nothing green, Easter still to come, crocus before and yellow forsythia after. Still, the seeds were there in the half-frozen ground and they were growing very nicely, thank you.

In the back of my mind there would sometimes blow a cold wind and I would shiver, for the wind said "Helen," the wind said "Brandon," and then the wind said "Simon," and "the jolly lecher."

What are you supposed to tell the man you are going to marry? What do you really know to tell him? That you feel like Miss Reject of nineteen oh nine and are afraid that he will reject you too? I had a secret or two but then surely so did Stanley; not the funny, silly secrets about petting in teenage cars or the embarrassments of having to go to the bathroom and not being able to say so when you are trying to be grand and grown-up with the boys from dancing school; not the social crises of having to admit you had used the wrong fork or upset your water glass in the middle of the table. We had told each other all these little bumps and bruises. What we had not told and seemed unable to tell were the times when we had been hurt to the heart and had bled copiously and had had no way to bind up the wound so that it could heal without leaving any scars.

Maybe it was just my cold wind, not his. Maybe he had no secrets like mine. I had to do something about my cold wind. I started by going to see Helen. It was a hard visitation to make. Her parting words of eleven o'clock wisdom had set my teeth on edge. Eleven o'clock will come indeed. Well, I had survived. Eleven o'clock had come and gone and here it was a quarter past midnight.

This visit Helen chose to receive me on the sunporch. She was busy doing découpage work and all the boxes of scraps and tinsel and wastepaper-basket emptyings were scattered about her wicker chair. On the table before her was her design for the day. I could not help the hostile thought that went before my hello. Would Helen never rise and come to meet me even halfway? Where was my hello kiss of welcome? I put my anger aside and gave her the homage kiss to her cheek. How cool the cheek, how sweet the face. Oh, it's a love and a hate together that make a cross child.

"You're working on something new, I see. What happened to the jigsaw puzzle?" Helen smiled enigmatic and unapproachable.

"Finished," she said, "long ago."

"What did it turn out to be?"

"I forget." Really, she was the most frustrating woman.

"What's all this, Helen?" I asked.

"Découpage." Helen was pleased. "I'll explain," she said, "you take all the scraps you can beg, borrow or steal and you make them into pretty things or at least the prettiest things you can manage to make."

"What's it going to be? What are you making?"

"Nothing concrete, nothing with a name," Helen said. "It's just mindless abstractions."

"Oh," I said, feeling more than ever like one of her mindless abstractions.

"How's your play? I hear you're very good."

"I'm fair in the play. We're closing soon."

"Holy Week, most likely," said Helen. "Holy Week does it every time. That and Christmas." She looked about her. "Do you see any bits of sponge?"

"There," I said, "in the box to the right."

"Hand it me, like a good girl." I hadn't been with her five minutes and she'd got me fetching and carrying. This had to stop.

"I'm getting married," I said.

"Good," Helen said, "and high time, too." She was absorbed in putting glue on the back of a small piece of sponge.

"What do you mean, high time?"

"You need someone to take care of you." Helen mopped up a drop of excess glue. "I never could and your father wouldn't." Then she looked at me. "Have you ever used Elmer's Glue? Really marvelous."

"No," I said, "I don't do much with glue. Do you want to hear about my love? His name is Stanley Partridge the Third."

"Sounds rich."

"He's not, he's poor. He has a lovely mother."

"Watch out for the old lady."

"You mean Mrs. Partridge? Not to worry, she's very nice and he's perfect."

"I'm not worrying," Helen said, "but watch out for the old lady all the same."

"I want you to meet him, Helen, but I don't want him cut up like your pretty bits."

"I doubt that you want me to meet him," Helen said. "I

rather imagine it's he who wants to meet me. With a name like that he must have conventions to follow."

"He hasn't asked to meet you, but it's got to be done."

"All right, then, bring him round. I'll be on my best behavior. We'll have tea. I'll get Eric to come. He's very good with the situation social. You'll see, Eric will find something for us to talk about that cannot possibly embarrass you. Eric is a very dear man."

"So is Stanley, so don't bite or frighten him."

"I told you I'd be good," Helen said irritably. "I'm not against your getting married, I really want you off my hands."

"And off your conscience?"

"Don't be rude to your mother," Helen said. "Look for some feathers and some sequins. They are all in together. I must sort it all out sometime. It would make my work easier if I did." I handed her the box.

"I have to go, I must," I said. "I have to meet Stanley."

"Then go," said Helen. I began to back away from her. "Diana," Helen said. She so rarely called me by my name that it brought me up short.

"What?"

"If you have any bits and pieces, you know, pretty bits of things you don't want you'll send them along to me, won't you?"

"Yes," I said, "I will."

"You promise?"

"Yes," I said, a lump in my throat, "I promise. I will send them." But I never did. One has to be punishing sometimes. One simply has to be. Because the old pain of loss is so great and the old threat of being left outside in the cold and the rain is too much to bear.

Brandon of course was another matter. I couldn't see flying out to California just so Stanley and Brandon the magnificent could play the "I beg the hand of your daughter scene"; neither did the gods for they blew a little luck my way. I read in the *Journal-American* that Brandon was in town taping a special television interview show for ABC.

How hard it is to communicate with one's father dear. It is easier to see the faceless face of the eternal God. Brandon was staying at the St. Regis. The desk clerk and switchboard had orders not to put any calls through.

"But," I said, "I'm his daughter."

"Bully for you," they said, "but Mr. Bradon says no calls." I was beside myself with frustration. I called the television studio. There they were on camera and tape central can be disturbed for no man.

I bethought myself of what to do. Should I write him a little pleading note? Should I stand about in the lobby and descend upon him like one of his female fans with an autograph book? Would it take a directive order from the President of the United States to put us in the same room? I had a sudden idea. I became hostile and sly. I called the hotel and asked for the manager. I pretended I was a long-distance operator. I informed the manager that I was Washington, D.C. I said I was the White House calling. I said I was secretary to the First Lady of the land and that the First Lady wanted to speak to Mr. Bradon about an official function in the nation's capital. Could, would the manager be a dear and get me Mr. Bradon on the line? He would, he could and he did. I got Brandon on the phone. He'd been in his suite all the time.

"Hello, Brandon," I said, "I had to go through channels to get you. How are you?"

"Marvelous," he said, "bloody marvelous."

"I'm bloody-minded," I said, and I told him the story of my difficulties in reaching him. He thought it was a hoot, the whole charade. He said he had intended to come to the theatre and surprise me afterward with his royal presence. He

said he would have gotten in touch with me but he thought
it might make me nervous to know he was out front.

I said I'd love for him to come to my play and I certainly
thanked him for being so considerate of my tender sensibili-
ties but that actually I was calling him about another matter
entirely.

"Why are you calling?" Brandon wanted to know, growing
suddenly suspicious. Did he think I wanted money or help
with my lifetime work?

"I'm getting married, Brandon," I said, "and I want you to
meet my young man." Brandon heaved a sigh of relief. I did
not want money.

"Certainly," he said, "glad to. Is he good enough for you?"

"Much too good, but don't tell him, it might frighten him
away."

"You know me better than that."

"I know you, Brandon, you are the Jack of Hearts."

"Thank you, daughter dear."

"You're welcome, father dear."

The conversation was over. All we had to do now was to
find a way to hang up. There was a considerable pause, much
heavy breathing.

"How's Helen?" he asked. "They won't let me talk to
her."

"She's fine Brandon, she really is."

"Good, good."

"How's your West Coast family, Brandon?"

"Couldn't be better."

"Good, good." What a rotten lot of dialogue. I must end
it at once. "How will we arrange this, Brandon? Where will
we meet you? Where will you be? My young man is shy."

"Oh." Pause while he thought that over. "I know," he said
at last, inspiration shedding light upon the two of us, "come
to the television studio. I finish up tomorrow, then back to
the Coast. Come at four, is that all right?"

"That's fine, what studio?"

"B–1 or B–12. Something like a vitamin. Anyway you can find it. You can find me, can't you?"

"Yes," I said, "I can always find you."

"Nice talking to you, Diana."

"Goodbye, father dear."

"Goodbye, daughter dear." I hung up. It wasn't impossible to find him, I had proved that. I felt old and wary beyond all my years.

The next day I took Stanley by the hand and off we went to ABC. I found the right building, the right floor, the right studio but Brandon had gone, vanished away. He had left a note. It said, "Have taken early plane to Coast. Domestic emergency. Sorry not to meet your intended. Will dance at your wedding."

Even a note in his own handwriting was not more than a hastily sent wire. He had tried to get in as many words as he could for the minimum fee. There was nothing that Brandon had ever said to me that could not have been said in ten words or less.

"Listen, Stanley," I said, "dear love. I'd love for you to meet my mother but I think maybe she's not feeling up to it just now. Can you understand?"

"Of course, is there anything I can do?"

"Yes," I said, "marry me please even though I think I'm a pig in a poke."

There was nobody left to tell but Simon. I had to tell Simon. One has to tell one's buddy chum pal that one is getting married. I mean it's only fair. We had written to each other faithfully if fitfully. But I could not write him this news. I telephoned. It was easier to get Simon in Ethiopia than to get Brandon at his hotel.

The connection was not so good. It crackled and snapped and hummed with the waves of the sea.

"Hello, hello, Simon. Are you there?"

"Diana, is it you?"

"Yes, Simon."

"What's up? Why the call?"

"Nothing really."

"Are you all right?"

"Oh, yes."

"What's the matter?"

"Nothing's the matter."

"What's the matter?"

"Nothing's the matter, I'm just getting married, that's all."

Snap, crackle, pop.

"Simon?"

"Yes."

"Did you hear me?"

"Yes."

Snap, crackle, pop.

"Say something, Simon."

"Don't do it, Diana."

"What?"

"Don't get married."

"Why not?"

"The gods will laugh."

"No, they won't. They won't even notice. They are **too** busy eating their dinner with you in Ethiopia."

"I'm serious, Diana. Dead serious."

"So am I."

Pop, waaaaash.

"Who are you going to marry?"

"No one you know."

"An actor?"

"No."

"Civilian."

"Yes."

"Are you determined to get married?"

"Yes."

"Well, then marry me."

Snap, pop, roar.

"What?"

"If you must marry, marry me."

"What for?"

Snap, crackle, pop, roar.

"Because we are buddy chum pals."

"No, Simon, not a good enough reason."

"Because we would both spoil two other couples."

"No, Simon."

"Because we are both permanently blighted."

"No, Simon, I'm not blighted, I'm walking now with the other wounded. You should see me walking. I walk very well, I really do."

Snap, crackle, pop, gigantic roar.

"Are you going to have a baby?"

"Yes, six at least."

"Please, Diana."

"Please, what?"

"Don't."

"Don't what?"

"Don't start the whole mess up again with a helpless baby."

Roar, snap, crackle, pop, snap.

"I don't hear you."

"Oh, Diana, if I had a human heart you'd break it half in two." Roaring and snapping and moaning the line went dead.

The connection was broken. I did not try to get Simon back again.

24

THE show was closing. The two week notice went up. Holy Week had worked its theatrical crucifixion. Soon we would set the date and post the banns when we would be married. I felt I had to say something to Stanley. I could not marry him and not say something and I did not know what to say.

He seemed so blissful, so uncomplicated. The sap in his veins flowing full spring tide, his eyes and skin and hair and nails were taking on new texture. Continence was getting further and further from our control. Physical contact was becoming a necessity. Our mouths were dry, our palms were hot, we could not eat our food, we left half-finished, savagely picked-over dinners uneaten in expensive restaurants all over town.

The tumult and the turmoil had to stop, had to be resolved. Our legs were made of glass and kept giving way at the knees. Our voices broke in adolescent hormonal tones. It really had to stop. I had it in mind to lure him to my lair. He had been avoiding the sublet and with good reason. It was full of furniture but all we saw was the bed. It kept being there, wherever we started out we invariably ended up by that big bed and Stanley would shy off and shoot out the door as if he had been given a lethal charge of negative electricity.

It had to stop. On the closing night of the play I used a

cover story of being tired and needing him to help me bring home my things from the dressing room as my bait. Stanley helped me carry my dressing case, my makeup case, and all my little hallmarks that I had acquired to travel me into strange theatres without feeling I was in a strange place. Home is where the hallmarks are. Helen had her little things and I had mine. I had once made fun of them but now I had my own collection, fragments with special meanings all their own. A bit of Brandon, a bit of Helen, a bit of Simon, a bit of the jolly lecher and now a bit of Stanley; pathetic objects that had no meaning for any individual except me. The baby has his ragged, dirty blanket, the businessman his company, the lonely lady all her rubies and diamonds and pearls. I had noticed that the sexually unresolved took mightily to star sapphires. There is a secret there in its depths but one had to hold it just so to see the flawed beauty.

"Are you sorry the play is closed?" Stanley asked me as he carted my silly totems from the elevator to the sublet door.

"No," I said, "I'm relieved. I told you that but you don't seem to believe it."

"Oh, I do," Stanley protested, "I believe you but I want you to have what you want." I opened the door and switched on the light.

"Put the things anywhere," I said. "Shove them behind chairs or sweep them under the rug. I'll get the mess sorted out later. I will, I promise you. I'm really neat at heart, you know, it's just the exterior."

"Just anywhere?" Stanley came inside the door but was tentative and shy. I closed the door behind him.

"I'm going to make us something to eat. I'm starved. It's hard work saying goodbye to an old way of life. It wears you out and makes you ravenous."

"I'll take you out to eat," Stanley said, darting for the door. "Where do you want to go?"

"Right here, home," I said, "right here. I do not want to ever eat in another restaurant as long as I live."

"Can you cook?" Stanley asked.

"Don't be a silly ass. Of course I can cook. What's there to cooking? Anyone who loves someone can cook. That's a trite scene from a plethora of playwrights."

"What?"

"The femme fatale saying to the man of the moment, 'I bet you'll be amazed to find I not only have sexual appetites, I have a stomach, too.' " Stanley winced. "Do I shock you?"

"No." I went on determined to have my way with Stanley or die in the attempt.

"Then there is the bride and all those terrible burned biscuits that follow as the day the night or the breakfast the night before or something." I stopped, a lump in my throat. I ached for him most terribly. "Stanley, why don't you make love to me?" Stanley looked all cornered and stricken. "Well, why don't you?" I pursued him. "I think you want to."

"I do."

"Then why don't you? Why are you smiling, Stanley?"

"Because."

"Tell me why?" I didn't understand him at all.

"Because I'm happy, I think."

"Well, I'm not happy. I want to lie down with you. Standing up all the time is a form of etiquette I can no longer endure."

"All right then," Stanley said. "It can't be wrong to want something so much, can it?"

"No," I said, "It can't be wrong."

We lay down quite peacefully together, Partridge and Bradon, lion and lamb, a little nervous, a little tentative but hopeful; too shy to be really satisfactory, but when we had time and the world enough we would be able to improvise upon the theme and make a tune or two of our own. I had faith in that. We lay afterward questioning in the dark.

163

"Are you all right?" Stanley asked me.

"Ummmmm hummmm."

"Ummm yes, or ummm no?"

"Ummm yes. Are you all right, Stanley?" I asked him.

"Yes."

"Anything else?"

"Yes."

"What?"

"Hungry. Didn't you say you could cook?"

"Yes."

"Then get up and prove it, woman, and stop all this incessant boasting." I cooked quite well, considering I had had no lessons.

But then sex wasn't everything we needed. Oh, wouldn't life be a simple dream if all you had to do to make life work out to an insured happy ending was just to adjust the flesh to the needs and the needing. One has to adjust the soul or the psyche or whatever it is as well and the two, those eternal twins, will travel around together constantly getting in each other's way.

My body was sort of almost all right with Stanley but my psyche-soul was very troubled and muddy. There was so much he did not know about me. I was so lacking and unworthy. I was so inadequate and insecure and he was so perfect and such a grand worthy deserving of nothing but the very best. It was so difficult and painful. I did care for him so, it seemed unfair to make him responsible for reclaiming such a depressed and unreclaimable area.

Now we were sleeping together, or at least lying down together, he kept pressing me to set the date. He wanted me to make an honest man of him and suddenly I did not know if I was equal to the task. In fact, I was damn sure I wasn't. He was much too good for me.

I became a television commercial of tension and anxiety; the brows knit up, the hands nervously twisting at my handkerchief or the handle of my handbag. I began to cry a lot, just sort of loose tears plopping down. I was an emotional atomic disaster area and they were my fallout. They fell all over Stanley. He tried to be a comfort.

"What is it, Diana? What is it, lovey dear?"

"It's me," I blurted. "I'm not any good at all."

"That's a silly thing to say. Why do you say a silly thing like that?"

"I'm not worthy of you."

"Why ever not? I'm the one that's no bargain."

"I have news for you, Stanley, I'm damaged goods."

"Even I notice some things, Diana. I gather you've been damaged but let me say as a Junior Expert that the goods are very good. I don't want to know about your past. I don't want to stir up what's gone before."

"What if I'm nobody, nothing at all, just a bag of theatrical tricks?"

"Let me decide, will you? You are someone for me. I wish you wouldn't make us talk. So much talking is very hard for me."

"All right, Stanley, I love you and I'll sleep with you and I won't make you talk, but I don't see how I can marry you." There, it was out at last.

"Why not?" Stanley was incredulous. "Why not, for the love of heaven?"

"Because," I sobbed, "I have no one to give me away. Helen's in the madhouse, Brandon's nowhere to be found. Now, you tell me how I can have a proper wedding when I've got no one to give me away."

"Is that all?" Stanley was relieved. "That's easily solved. You pretend that you are an orphan and I'm Daddy Longlegs and I'll give you a wedding." I howled and plopped a lot of tears. "Sorry," Stanley said, "I just wanted to make a joke. There, there, never mind, we'll fiddle up a wedding now and very soon."

Stanley's solution to the wedding crisis was to have his mother give us away. It wasn't proper Partridge protocol but it was a solution. She loved it. She took over like Gangbusters, breaking up the bootleggers' saloon. Well, it was a way of shifting the responsibility of the wedding onto Stanley. I did not know that at the time but I was sort of saying "This is something I'm not up to but since you insist, why then take it upon your head and so be it. You be responsible for me."

Stanley was responsible. Certainly his mother was more in a position to function than mine. Mrs. Partridge even managed to get Brandon to show up on the appointed day in a cutaway and striped trousers, which is more than Helen could have done. Mrs. Partridge arranged for the wedding to take place in June in the garden of the gamekeeper's cottage.

There were clouds on the morning of the wedding and it looked like rain, but by noon we stood under the rose arbor and promised to love, honor and obey each other till death us did part, no man putting us asunder. The sun shone, the roses bloomed, the caterers catered without any flaw on this most flawless of days. There was only one bad moment. The minister did ask if anyone knew of any impediment to our union, let him speak now or forever hold his peace and I felt that I should raise my hand.

The great and the near-great had come out bidden by the Partridge name and mixed among them like wild and gaudy field flowers among hothouse plants were the remains of my theatrical acquaintances. My, they did stand out, especially my agent, who spoke his fractured French to the French Ambassador.

Brandon charmed them all, shook hands with them all, danced with all the ladies. It really was a lovely wedding. I was sorry that Helen could not have come, she had bought a new dress and had a special outpatient's pass for her good behavior; then at the last minute she had gotten to the gate and could not come out. Mr. Margolies had stayed with Helen and surely that was a relief for him, because he had not thought it absolutely right to appear if Brandon was going to be there and yet he had wanted to come in case Brandon had turned out to be a no-show. He said he had wanted someone to give me away. Was that not the nicest thought that Mr. Margolies had ever had for me? That was quite wedding present enough without his sending some family silver and a handsome check.

Brandon's most precious gift to me was not on the display tables. He was splendid, he really was. He did not wig it or wing it, he came on straight with the gray in his hair. How white it was getting and how all the bald spots were beginning to shine through. It made me sad to see what a thief time had been with him. He would never have appeared so naked in public if he were not aware of growing a little old. I would rather in a way that he had ogled the ladies and made them flutter. I would rather he had drunk too much and quoted from Shakespeare than to see that while my back was turned he had passed middle age and gone toward winter.

Oh, but he was a grand old man entirely when he walked us down the aisle of roses together and gave me into Stanley's hand. It must have meant something to him because he was trembling. Stanley was handsome, steady and resolute, a prince of a fellow. I was a lucky, lucky girl, all the guests said so.

The ceremony was done, the cake was cut, we led the dancing, Stanley and I, and true to his word Brandon cut in on us and danced with me, his darling daughter on her wedding day. He hugged me to him all hoarse and red-eyed and he said:

"You may not believe I love you but I do." I could not bear the pain. True, he had come for my wedding day, but where had he been all my life? It seemed to me that he had come too late.

I ran away to change into my traveling costume. I threw the bouquet to the assembled throng. They threw rice and Stanley and I slipped away in a shower of rice and roses. I had just what I wanted, a real life of my own. I had a moment of guilt because I missed Simon so but I really could not have expected him to come all the way from Ethiopia for the nuptials.

Stanley and I sailed away to Europe for our honeymoon because all Partridges sailed away to Europe on their honeymoons, it was a family tradition. But unlike most Partridges it was on my honeymoon that I first suspected that I was going mad.

25

I FEARED I was going mad because when I spoke to Stanley he did not seem to hear me. We seemed to be having a gigantic aural misunderstanding. He heard other people, therefore he was not deaf, but when I spoke he did not hear me. I began to doubt that I had really spoken at all.

"Do you hear me speaking to you?" I asked Stanley at last, when I could bear it no longer.

"Yes," Stanley said slowly and thoughtfully, "I hear you." I knew there was more he was not saying. When pressed Stanley admitted that while he heard the words I spoke, he regretfully did not always understand their meaning. He said it sounded rather like code and that he had no key. Stanley looked perplexed.

I said not to worry, it must be my fault because, as everyone knew, code was to confuse the enemy and certainly Stanley was not the enemy, and he said he hoped not.

I must not have been hearing him properly either because he said he had told me that the reason such a poor Partridge as he could afford a European honeymoon was that it was a business trip. The Foundation was going to pick up the tab. I had not thought that a honeymoon should be tax-deductible and come off the expense account.

That was the beginning. Then came the jokes. I'd make a little joke and Stanley wouldn't laugh, he would not even smile. I'd say, "Stanley, that was a little joke."

And he'd say, "Why is it a joke?" and I'd have to explain why it was a joke. I stopped speaking to Stanley unless I was sure he would understand. I stopped making jokes altogether.

Not that I was miserable or anything like it. Both Stanley and I were very happy in an unhappy sort of way. We had a fabulous time on the nuptial journey. We went to Ireland and oh, it was green. We went to Scotland and looked at the lochs. We went to London, a far different London than I had seen in my funny hat. Stanley was a member of everything or had a member's privileges. We went to the country to see the stately homes, only this time I did not have to pay two and six. This time I was inside with the family looking out at the tourists.

We went to Paris where Stanley was kissed by a general and I spent a fortune for one dress and looked at pictures until I went colorblind. We drove through France eating and drinking all the way. I felt the need of doing some useful work between meals, so I began a treatise on the relative merits of Béarnaise sauce of the various regions; then on to Italy where we had an audience with the Pope and where I saw myself in the cinema in *The Last Days of Delilah* and discovered I had been dubbed into Italian.

We flew to Greece where Stanley lectured me on the Athenians and the Spartans and read aloud from Thucydides and where we bobbed up and down endlessly in a small boat on the wine-dark sea.

My husband was a good sailor, a gentleman, a cheerful traveling companion and a complete stranger to me. I could not make him out. Trying to understand Stanley became an obsession. I stared at him as if he were an exhibit in a glass case. He was delicious to see, as pink and brown as a wildly expensive suit in Hattie Carnegie's window, and beyond my reach as a display or royal jewels at Van Cleef and Arpels.

He was everlastingly polite. How, when everything was so

terrible, could he be so patiently polite? I wanted to kick and scream, rampage against the days we spent without speaking, without comprehending, living in a dungeon of misunderstanding, and all Stanley did was to be polite.

In our bed at night there was a ritual, a courtesy so exquisitely polite I thought it must be a joke. In the bed where there should be no thought, only a surfeit of feeling, I thought a series of disconnected thoughts which at last made me want to giggle more than scream. Ours was undoubtedly a functional bed, a functional piece of furniture, a functional marriage serving a purpose and functioning properly without any unnecessary nonsense.

How could Stanley be so polite and cheerful and lie in the same bed with such loneliness? He seemed not to notice that we were out of touch. Could it be that Stanley was content? Was this what he had expectantly bargained for? If that was true, my situation was even worse than I imagined. If this was all there was between husband and wife, if we had been made one flesh till death us did part and this was indeed the more perfect union, then I had been badly misled. There must be something more. This could not be all there was to reality.

Yes, Stanley seemed to find it enough and more than enough. He went on day after day, one step in front of another, looking as pleased and as happy as a bridegroom should be.

I felt I must find some way to communicate with Stanley about what seemed to be my personal problem. I had to find out if this was the good and happy life we were living. If so, I must adjust to the facts, for the honeymoon was nearly over.

I thought it best to approach the subject on neutral ground. I was afraid to bring it up when we were alone, for fear of my reaction. If I asked in a crowd, I would have to behave myself no matter what the answer. I must ask soon, time was short.

Greece was the end of the trip to the East. Here we faced about toward the West and started for home. As a concession to my craving for Béarnaise sauce, I was to be allowed a last meal in Paris. An airplane flying from Athens to Paris seemed to be a safe forum. I tugged at Stanley's sleeve. He had been looking out the window gazing at the clouds. He turned his smooth, untroubled face to me.

"Are you happy, Stanley?"

"Of course I am."

"Do you think I am?"

"I hope so."

"What if we were both miserably, wildly unhappy?"

Stanley smiled. "I think," he said, "that I love you more than you love me." Did he think I had made one of my jokes?

"Wouldn't that make you unhappy?" I asked.

"But we aren't unhappy," he said with an air of confidence.

"But what if we were?" I prodded.

"Why," Stanley said with some conviction, "we'd have to try and get over it."

I started to protest but Stanley had not finished his forensic. He proceeded with what I came to think of as basic Partridge philosophy. Stanley said that unhappiness, according to the gospel of Partridge, was entirely unnecessary. Of course, if one lacked material and economic necessities that was one thing. Then, of course one should seek some remedy but most people, Stanley said, brought unhappiness upon themselves. They looked for it, used their leisure time to stir up discontent in themselves. The thing to do, Stanley said, was to get on with one's job and not go about looking for imperfection, for in this imperfect world one was sure to find it. Do your work, that was Stanley's motto. Work was everything. Did I not agree?

I stared at Stanley, speechless. Work was nothing to me if I had no one to love.

"Well," Stanley said, putting his hand over mine and giving it a squeeze, "we'll be in Paris for dinner."

I was being allowed a last fling in Paris for my good behavior. While in Greece I had discovered that I was pregnant. At first I had thought it was all the bobbing up and down on the Aegean that had made me feel so odd but it was more than mal de mer.

The promise, the purpose of our trip by all real-life standards had been brilliantly fulfilled. I was to be fruitful and multiply. I was going to have something for me and no cause to ever feel discontented again. The honeymoon was over; one quick, last look at Paris and home.

I did not enjoy Paris. It seemed futile to buy clothes I could not wear. I had seen the galleries. Food was of less than general interest to me. I was evidently determined to be original and theatrical in every way. I was not sick in the morning. In the mornings I felt fine. I was sick in the afternoon. Every afternoon at five o'clock I was sick as a chien. It made for a simply hideous dinner hour. Then about ten o'clock I began to rally and by eleven o'clock I was ready for an after-the-theatre supper. Stanley could not eat that late at night. It gave him indigestion and kept him awake.

I did not care. We were leaving Paris the next day to sail for the new world. Before I left for the great unknown, before I was the hostage of the Partridges, before the baby took complete possession of me, I wanted to be humored. I wanted to be pampered. I wanted to be taken to the top of Montmartre and be fed an enormous bifteck with gobs of Béarnaise sauce. I had finished the packing. I was going home without making a scene. The least Stanley could do was to humor me.

Stanley agreed but there was a beam and a mote in his eye which told me he was only pleasing me now in the surety that soon I must humor him. Well then, tonight I would drink the last of the wine and tomorrow I would remember to walk softly, speak distinctly and make no jokes. We had such a long walk to make through life together.

We went up to Madame Recamier's. Madame Recamier was a great, fat Negress who lay on a chaise longue in her bistro, under the shadow of the Sacré Coeur. When the mood was upon her, she could still sing a song to break your heart. She had been lying there since the days of Hemingway and Stein and all those expatriated young people.

She was not in the mood for singing every day, so those who came to see her had to provide some entertainment of their own. It was very gay. There was always a singing and dancing at Madame Recamier's.

As we came in a young man in a beard with a lute on his back was going out. We bumped into each other, touched and drew apart without my seeing his face clearly. Stanley, protective, snapped at him.

"Here, look where you're going," but the young man with the lute went on past and paid Stanley no mind.

I stood quite still. I felt sure that it was Roland. I wanted to run after him and ask if he were indeed the long-lost Roland but I could not move.

"Are you all right?" Stanley asked.

"Yes."

"Anything the matter?"

"No."

I could not tell Stanley anything that mattered because he would not hear me. It was very sad not being able to tell. If you know and are with someone you cannot tell it to, it's like being with no one at all. You are more lonely than all alone.

That last night in Paris the Béarnaise sauce was not to my liking. There was too much tarragon, the herbs were bitter to the taste. For a lifetime we were sentenced to eat all our meals together and I sat at the table of the enemy.

O NCE home from the honeymoon it became painfully apparent that the beam and the mote were in my eye. That it was I and not Stanley that was the enemy. It seemed that whatever I wanted and hoped for would not do. Stanley was forced to point out to me that I was not thinking like a proper Partridge wife. He seemed saddened by the necessity of having to have this little heart-to-heart talk with me. I'm sure he had thought I would make the transition from Bradon to Partridge with no effort at all. It was so obvious that the change of identities was all to my advantage.

Sadly, sadly, Stanley approached his erring wife with tact and patience. He laid out the path that all Partridge women must walk. There was a right way, a wrong way, and a Partridge way. It seemed to me that they were all without laughter. It seemed that I kept wandering off onto the grass. I could never, never tell what was grass and what was path.

I had hoped to live in a Greenwich Village apartment, something large and loft-like with a glorious skylight. I had thought to buy an enormous bed and put it beneath the skylight so that while we made love we might watch the stars and the running lights of airplanes on their night flights.

I wanted a place on my own that I could fill with expendable furniture from the Salvation Army, and burlap drapes and multi-colored crockery; a place I could care for myself while I learned some housewifely skills, and discovered what our more permanent tastes in period furniture might be; a place on Jane Street or in a mews or up an alley; a place where I could make a lot of mistakes that would not cost too much and that could be erased when we found a larger apartment after the baby came.

I had somehow gotten it into my head that a baby in a loft might be fun for a while. What do babies need but a crib, a lot of sunshine and milk and cuddles before you make them dry and give them their naps. The sun shines through a skylight the same as it does in a park, or so I thought. But the Village would not do as a suitable address for a Partridge Foundation Junior Expert. Stanley's mother pointed this out to Stanley and me. She most graciously insisted that we take her dower house, hunting lodge in Tarrytown. She was more than willing to move to an apartment hotel between Madison and Park in the east Sixties since, as she said, she had no son to keep house for now.

So Mrs. Partridge went to town and I went to Tarrytown to live in her house. She left a lot of her things behind in closets and drawers and cellars and attics. Stanley said it was only sensible because she had no storage room where she was going and certainly in a house this size there was room for all our things.

He was right. I brought very little with me. I had no need to even unpack my linens or blankets or tablecloths. All the necessary furnishings were provided by Mrs. Partridge. For me it was just like another sublet, only much more grand.

When Mrs. Partridge came for Thanksgiving and Christmas and Easter and birthdays and odd Sundays and weekends, she sorted over all her things and allowed me to tell her at least once a visit how grateful I was for her sacrifice.

"There is something wrong with my character," I said to Stanley.

"Why?" he said, loving brown eyes upon me.

"Because," I said, "I say I'm grateful to your mother but I don't really feel grateful. I'm really not if I'm honest."

"Well," said Stanley, wrinkle-browed, "no matter how you feel, if someone has given you a present you should thank them, don't you think? I mean when you are handed something you must accept it gracefully."

"Yes," I said, "I see what you mean. I'll try, really I will."

The house was too big, the furniture was not mine, the remnants of the woman too many to be cared for handily by me. I hated the house, it smelled of her. When I walked in the door I smelled her, when I opened a closet the scent of her overpowered me. Stanley said he thought his mother was a peach to let us use the house and didn't I agree and I said yes I did, a living peach, and I hugged him close as I could for fear he might not love me if I told the truth.

If I were truthful I'd have to say I hated that house. We moved into it on Halloween and from that night on it was one long spook show that I came to think of as the Tarry-town tumble, or a tiny tragedy in three yearly acts; a charade of masks and monsters that must to the rest of the world have looked like the rich, full life, full of blessings, while to me with my one eye of love it was a living death.

The first year the death was not so bad, except I had too much time. I was not used to the way time was told in the land of the Partridge. They did not seem to mark the passing of time with regret, they regarded it as the natural sequence of things. Partridges were born, grew up, went to school, traveled, went to work, married, had children, grew older, played with their grandchildren, grew older still and died. They had their share of sudden death or disaster and accident but it was the exception to their rule, it left their main pattern unruffled and unmuddied.

I had not been used to living in days or weeks or months, certainly not in years or the circle of a lifetime. Time to me had been a quarter of an hour, a change of costume in fifteen minutes. Thirty years could elapse between the first and second acts of a play and only fifteen minutes had ticked off the real clock. Each day I had one performance or two or a meeting or a letter to write or Simon to see. I missed Simon, I missed having a buddy chum pal to talk to. I felt it disloyal to Stanley to miss Simon so.

"Listen," I said to Stanley.

"I'm listening."

"Can we be friends?"

"We are friends," Stanley said, "aren't we?"

"Yes," I said slowly, "maybe I mean pals, buddy chum pals." Stanley smiled, his brown eyes went far away.

"I had a pal at school. We went all through school and camp together. Wonderful fellow. Did I ever tell you about him?"

"No." I felt I was not communicating at all. Stanley told me all about his pal. He said one day he would like me to meet him and I said I would like to.

But still the first year was not so very bad. Even with whole days in which I had nothing to do, in which I was an inmate in a hell of nothingness, I managed to survive. Even Mrs. Partridge was able to put my failures down to the effects of pregnancy. The baby was growing away unmindful of my predicament. It grew and kicked and shoved and jabbed with its knees and elbows. I was merely an accommodation station. Not that it mattered. I liked having the baby. It was something to look forward to; the euphoria of gestation, like a daily dose of morphine, saved me from realizing how mortal my wound of discontent really was.

I was pregnant, there was no need to be anything else. I had a part-time housekeeper, a part-time laundress, a part-time gardener, all hired by Mrs. Partridge. My marvelous device of avoidance was sleep. I slept almost all the time.

And when I was not asleep I went to natural childbirth exercise classes, which Mrs. Partridge made great fun of to my face and told Stanley were unhealthy behind my back. I was angry with her, which made me feel guilty. I thought of all my theatrical days and took Mrs. Partridge to lunch at Sardi's to prove I could still get a table without a reservation. Mrs. Partridge said we should have gone to the Plaza where it was not so noisy and crowded and where she was known.

I took Mrs. Partridge home to her town apartment in a taxi wishing that I did not have to go home to Tarrytown to her house. I went to meet Stanley at his office. He said he thought I looked depressed and he would take me out to dinner and cheer me up.

"I know," he said, an idea popping into his head like an electric sign from above, "why don't we go to Sardi's. I miss the cannelloni," but I said no, I'd rather go to the Plaza. We had a miserable evening, Stanley very glum because as it turned out Stanley hated the Plaza, his father having taken him there on state occasions when he was a child.

I felt oppressed and harried and pushed, which was silly because the only thing I had to do was to sit in Tarrytown and wait for Stanley to call and tell me where to meet him for dinner or cocktails or tell when his mother was coming out for the weekend.

Stanley was very busy, reclaiming and evaluating depressed areas. He had to travel about and make reports on what he saw. He kept a bag packed in his office so he did not have to come home at all before he went to the airport if he did not want to. He could just call from the office and say, "I'm taking the night flight for . . ." and name a place a world away.

His mother called me once a day to see how Stanley was and I said he was fine and then she asked how the baby was growing and I said just fine thank you and then as an afterthought she would ask me how I was and I'd always say just fine, thank you, which was a lie but I had no frame of reference for real life and I thought this might be all there was to it and I had said that I wanted a real life with all my heart.

Mrs. Partridge called to see if I wanted to join the Junior League and I said, "No thank you." Mrs. Partridge had her feelings hurt, you could hear the hurt feelings over the silence of our connection. I brooded over her call, I did not want to be ungrateful or ungracious. I called Stanley to ask him what he thought. I wanted to know if he thought I should join to please his mother or not join to please me. His secretary said he was in a board meeting. I asked his secretary to give him a message that Mrs. Partridge had called. His secretary said that she had interrupted the board meeting not five minutes ago to say that Mrs. Partridge had called and I said to please tell him that this message was from Mrs. Partridge the Queen Wife not Mrs. Partridge the Queen Mother.

Stanley was forced to tell me in a heart-to-heart way that he did not think my message was funny nor did his secretary. I stopped trying to cut any capers or play the foolish part. I was not funny any more, no doubt about it. Once I had thought I was funny. Surely the audiences that had roared like a great beast with a feather in its ribs at the girl in the peekaboo hat had not all been so very wrong, or had they really ever laughed at all? Had I only imagined the laughter? I felt more than a little mad. I did not know what was what any more. The baby was getting enormous. I had heartburn. I had cramps in my legs, first my right leg and then my left.

I knew what it must be like to come home to me because I knew what I was like at home. I knew that much. When Stanley came home he was tired and I was not tired but I was bored.

"Shall we go out?" Stanley would ask bewildered by his fatigue and my boredom.

"No," I said, thinking to please him, "I want to stay in."

"Shall we stay in?" Stanley would ask, benumbed by his desire to please me.

"No, let us go out," but he did not want to go out, he had just come in and I did not want to come in or go out for I was nowhere, isolated, cut off, estranged, alienated from every creature on earth. Nothing I did seemed to make the smallest difference. I did try. I ate nicely at the table or as nicely as I was able, until the food stuck in my throat and the tears began to form in my one good peekaboo eye.

"Stanley," I said, trying not to look at him over the candelabra, trying not to make a scene in front of the servants. "Stanley," I said, "does it occur to you that our life is a terrible parody of a terrible soap opera?"

"I don't think so," Stanley replied chewing evenly and swallowing with apparent ease. "We are in the top ten per cent of the nation."

"I'm in the lower ten per cent of despair." Stanley stopped chewing.

"Oh, Diana, please. What do you want me to do? Tell me and I will do it."

"Nothing," and I cried.

"Oh, Diana, please don't cry." I cried all the more. And at night when we were in bed and Stanley was fast asleep I cried with both eyes. I cried rivers. One eye cried tears of self-pity and one eye cried tears of terror, for if I told Stanley what I wanted I would say that what I wanted was for him to take me away from all this and all this was just where he himself had brought me. This was his real life that he was sharing with me as the baby was sharing mine. I must be a silly, pregnant, overemotional girl, a very bad case of arrested development. I should be arrested, that was certain and made to stop whatever it was that I was doing or not doing. I deferred trying to find out what it was that I was doing or leaving undone until the baby came. It was a life deferred.

The baby would not defer its life, the baby was born when

it was ready, which was prematurely. My baby was a girl. We named her Sarah after some long-vanished Partridge and Helen for mum.

I could not have had better medical care. The baby was delivered by the Partridge family obstetrician at the Beecher Pavilion. I had hoped to go to Ladies' Lying In which encouraged natural childbirth and babies in their own mothers' rooms but Stanley's mother told him that having babies was no foolish matter. She told him he would never know how brave she had been when he was born, how valiant it was of her not to scream and disturb the other patients. She said even if I did not feel pain like she did I ought to have proper medical care. I knew I was a peasant to her and not a princess and peasants are not supposed to be like the ladies of the castle, still I objected in my own feeble way.

"Listen," I said to Stanley, "I don't want to go to the Beecher Pavilion, it's miles from anywhere."

"It's quiet," Stanley said thoughtfully.

"I want to go to Ladies' Lying In where they don't leave you alone in the dark and they let you drink cups of tea and there is a fireplace in every room."

"Is that hospital sanitary?"

"No, but it's cheerful and it doesn't smell of ether and oblivion."

"I think you ought to go to the Pavilion."

"Why?"

"What if something happened?"

"What can happen, it's just a baby being born."

"Something terrible. I don't want to be responsible for your being in agony without the proper care."

I was properly cared for. I had a sitting room and a bedroom. I had special nurses for me and for Sarah. They wouldn't let me see her at first because she was not able to breathe properly. They put her in a glass incubator and kept her in a glass nursery.

My sitting room and bedroom were full of flowers and Partridges. I had not known there were so many of either in the world. Mrs. Partridge presided. She said I must not worry about the baby being early. No one would think the less of me, lots of Partridge babies were early.

I had telegrams and presents all so like an opening night, only the real star was down the hall and behind glass. The assembled throng all trooped down the hall to see her. I was too weak even to look for a few days and had to make do with hearsay accounts. Everyone said I had a lovely baby.

Stanley came to the hospital every day for the first three days and every day he said that Sarah was acceptable, beautiful and perfect, what he could see of her. The third day he said that he had to go to South America to make a report on rainfall in the Pampas. I held his hand.

"Don't go."

"I hate to go, you know that."

"Stay."

"I must go, it's my job."

"Stay."

"Why, what is it? What may I get you?"

"I'm hungry."

"Haven't they brought you your dinner?"

"Yes, I'm still hungry."

"There's a dining room, you can order any time. I must go now or miss my plane." Stanley kissed me and left.

I turned my face to the wall. I was very ill in the night. The floor nurse sent for the doctor. He came at once.

"What is it? Where does it hurt?" I covered my heart as if I were saluting the flag. It was beating in a great terror tempo.

"Here," I said, "and there and everywhere."

"What can I do for you?"

183

"I want someone to take care of me."

"Now don't be a silly girl. I'm here, I'm taking care of you." He gave me a sedative. The next morning the doctor came again. "Now," he said, "how are you today?"

"I'm just fine, thank you," I said and I burst into tears.

"Postpartum depression," he said. "I'll prescribe an anti-depressant."

I went home to Tarrytown to an empty house with a jar of pink happy-pills clutched in my hot little Stanleyless hand. Sarah had to stay in the hospital until she was a bit larger. In a week or so she came home with her nurse who did not really like me to play with Sarah and who on her day off left me complete typewritten instructions for motherhood. Stanley came home from South America only to come and go and come and go again.

The second year I settled into a deeper despair. Even a pill a day did not keep the despair away. Stanley's mother said I looked peaked and must get out more. She said I should sit on more committees. Stanley said he thought I was bored and didn't I think I should go back to work?

I went into town to see my agent who said he would start looking around for something really worthy of my talents and meanwhile why didn't I go over and see about the Bliss commercial. They were looking for a Bliss girl and it just might be me.

"What's Bliss?" I asked him. He looked pained.

"And you a housewife?" he said. "It's for dishes or floors or something. Anyway it's changing color and they want a girl to lend product identification. A young housewife under twenty to show that Bliss has now gone modern and has a new look."

"It's soap," I said.

"Yes," he said, "that's it. Soap."

I went to see the Bliss people. The ad agency was full of a lot of girls wanting to be Miss Bliss, wanting to be under twenty and the American dream of Miss Happy Home-maker. I was handed some copy marked "Top Secret." The secret was that Bliss had gone from old-fashioned white to new think-pink. It was now so pink and mild that it could wash all your cares away.

I was suddenly very cold; the buildings of Madison Avenue are all air-conditioned, you cannot open a window in any of them, not even if you are suffocating. The temperature is always mortuary cold. I was in a panic. I had a presentiment that Sarah was in danger, and that I was needed at home. I handed back the copy to the receptionist.

"I can't say here," I said. "I'm needed at home."

If anything happened to Sarah and I was not there I would die. I knew the nurse was reliable. She told me so and she had references to prove it, but if anything happened and I was not there, I would be responsible and I had to be very responsible for Sarah. I had to keep her safe. I had to go home. I had to make a home for Sarah and for Stanley in case he ever came home to stay. That was my work, my real life, not playing dress-up on the stage or being Miss Bliss. I could not leave or we would all be in great danger. I did not know in danger of what precisely but we would be in terrible danger. I rushed to the train and I hurried home.

I ran into the nursery prepared for disaster. Sarah was fine, standing in her crib, nine months of fun. She had a new tooth. I picked her up and hugged her to me in gratitude and relief. I whispered in her ear.

"I've failed with everything else, please don't let me fail with you." I hugged her too hard and she cried.

Stanley came home to dinner unexpectedly. We ate in silence. As we drank our coffee I said, "I went to read for a television commercial."

"Good," Stanley said, "when do you go to work?"

"I'm not going to work," I said. "I can't go to work, Stanley." He looked bewildered.

"Why not?"

"Because," I said, "we are in terrible danger. I've been wanting to talk to you about our terrible danger but you are never here."

"What is it?" Stanley grew concerned. "What's happened?"

"Nothing," I said, "that's the danger we are in. Nothing is happening and time is going by so quickly. If we don't do something about it right now, today, every minute, we are going to die and nothing will ever have happened in our whole lives."

"I'll get you a brandy," he said sternly.

"I don't want a brandy," I said. "I want to stay at home and take care of Sarah. Can't you see I'm afraid something will happen to her?"

"Yes," he said, "but I think you may be hysterical, too." I cried. "You don't understand." I said, "We're going to fall over a cliff and you don't see the danger."

"Is all this because you don't want to go back to work?"

"Yes," I said. "No," I said. "Oh, please listen."

"I'm listening and if you don't want to go back to work," he said slowly, "then you don't have to but I think you are going to regret it."

"All right," I sobbed, "but I can't leave home, I just can't."

Stanley persevered at his work. He was asked to be the principal speaker at a Partridge Foundation dinner where they gave an accounting of the millions they had spent to better the world. Stanley's mother called to say this was the second year she had not gone with him.

Stanley and I sat at the highest table. Stanley introduced me to the wife of the Chairman of the Foundation as his wife who used to be an actress.

"And how is Mrs. Partridge?" the Chairman's wife asked me. "She's done such wonderful things for Stanley."

"Mrs. Partridge the wife or Mrs. Partridge the Queen Mother?" I asked and nearly bit out my tongue for shame. Stanley looked stricken and the Chairman's wife looked startled.

I could not wait to get home where, when Stanley was asleep and could not see my face, I could cry to my heart's content. I had put off asking any more questions until the baby was born and then I had put off asking any questions because I was afraid of what the answers might be and here it was in a dark hour of the night and the questions could not be put off any longer. Something must be the matter with me if I was so discontent. Whatever it was, it was too much for me to study alone. I thought of Helen in her madhouse.

27

I WAS afraid I must be mad too, freezing to death in a land of snow and ice. There was a great gap in my glacier world. It must be me. I was a bottomless pit of ice, no way to fill me up or thaw me out. Everyone everywhere was behind glass and the glass was made of ice. It must be my fault that I could not love them enough to melt the ice and glass between us.

I could not even reach Sarah. I felt that I did not love her enough and that she knew it. To make up for my lack I played and played with Sarah. I wore her out playing with her, singing her songs and teaching her rhymes. I sang and sang. I sang "Buy Me Blue Ribbons." "Oh dear, oh dear, what can the matter be? . . . He promised to buy me blue ribbons and yet he's so long at the fair?" As I sang to Sarah I began to cry.

"I don't like that song," Sarah said.

Neither did I.

Stanley was busier and busier. He ran and ran, my beautiful gingerbread boy. I was the fox after all and now he was busy running away from me. I went to bed too early, too tired. He came to bed too late, too tired. We lay in bed in silence. No matter what I did he would never make a sound. He never heard me speaking. He surely must be dissatisfied with that bed. Sometimes he shook me by the shoulders wanting a response to a sound he never heard. I began to sleep again. I slept and slept and would not get out of bed.

"You must get up," Stanley said, "if only to say goodbye."

"Are you going?"

"Yes," he said, "I must go out and work."

"I'm sick," I said.

"Then you must go to the doctor. What seems to be the matter?"

"I'm fine," I said. "I'm really fine. I just can't get out of bed."

"Why not?"

"I'm too tired."

The doctor made a lot of tests. He said I had low blood pressure, a low thyroid and was anemic. He said I needed a vacation.

"I'm too tired to go to the airport. Besides, my sinus is giving me a lot of trouble. Maybe that's what's wrong with me."

The doctor gave me some thyroid pills, some iron capsules and a decongestant. I took them home and put them on the bathroom shelf next to the pink anti-depressant pills.

"Am I going to die?" I had asked him as I had left his office.

"Silly girl."

"I feel like dying," I had said as I left his office. "I feel like death."

The third year the gray, green, greasy life-sickness settled upon me. Despair is always measurable. It is or was to me, the difference between what you have and what you want. My despair was small and round and gray. It had hairs on it and I could not get it up or down. I stayed at home and never went out. I made a doll's house for Sarah. It took up all my time. I worked on it night and day. It became a mania. I sent out for more and more materials to make Sarah's doll's house the most special and beautiful thing I

189

could create. I filled the nursery with boxes of pretty things, sequins and beads and silks and feathers and damasks. I made each piece of furniture. I painted every picture. I had never worked so hard in my life. No production, no role had ever been as difficult and yet I could not finish the house.

I had no time for Stanley. I could not even eat with him. I had my suppers on a tray and had gone to bed before he came home, or I said I was too busy to eat with him and stayed up long after he had gone to bed. It became a game of lifetime proportions. I must finish the doll's house and yet if I did I would have to play Nora and slam the door on my house of despair. I could not stop working and I could not finish. I could not leave the nursery.

Stanley came to the nursery, a suitcase in hand.

"Are you going, Stanley?"

"Yes," he said, "why should I stay?"

"I need you."

"I'm going to Asia Minor and I won't be home for a long time."

I started to cry.

"I must have my work. I must have something."

"You'll find a girl there in Asia Minor and you'll stay with her forever and have seven children under the age of six."

"I must have something."

"Stay here," I said, "speak to me. Be my friend. Play with us, with Sarah and me. I'm making such a pretty doll's house."

"No," Stanley said, "I'm going. It's my job."

"Why don't you get another?"

"I can't just quit. That would be like my father, who just quit and went away. The Foundation is my job. My mother made a sacrifice of herself to get me this job. I have a responsibility to my mother, to you, to Sarah. I can't just quit."

"You said you'd live with me."

"God knows I've tried but you are never available."

"I'm always here."

"Not to me."

"Then go," I said.

"I'm going," Stanley turned toward the door.

"Did it ever occur to you that you are being like your father and leaving me like he left her?"

"What a thing to say. I've never left you."

"You've never been here."

"When did I leave you?"

"On the honeymoon, I think."

"You're mad." Stanley was cornered by the door and angry. "You're like your mother and father. You're mad as a hatter."

I laughed.

"What's funny?" Stanley demanded.

"I'm mad all right. You're quite right. I'm the girl in the peekaboo hat and as mad as a peekaboo hatter." Stanley was out of all patience.

"I can't talk now. I have a plane to catch. Say something so that I can go. Diana, say something to me."

"Goodbye, Stanley."

He went away. I sat and shook with a fear that had led to a present trembling. My despair was greater than it had ever been.

I stopped working on the doll's house. There was something missing from that house. No matter how hard I worked I could not find out what it was that kept that house from being perfect. I looked at it hour after hour. In all its pretty well-made beauty there was a flaw. I wanted to tear it all apart and begin again because there was something missing. I had done that before, I had torn it apart and begun again. This time I must find the missing piece of the puzzle.

I put the family of dolls on the grass in front of the house and I gazed and gazed at all I had made of the pretty bits. And then I looked at the family, the mother doll and the children. I thought of Beatrix Potter's tale of the two bad mice and I yearned for a policeman to come and guard the house while I went away to life. There was something missing and no way to find it unless I advertised. I began to think of an advertisement to put in the *New York Times*. If I could advertise my pain and my loss in the *Times* then no one could doubt my tale then, for they printed all the news that was fit to print.

I found a pencil and paper and wrote out my complaint. It read ONE LOVELY LADY OF LONELYVILLE NEEDS HELP. No, that would not do. That was Help Wanted. LOST LADY IN SUBURBS WEEPS HAS LOST HERO TO COMFORT HER. No, that was Lost and Found. I needed another category for my one-line squib. Did they have a column for Miracles? Such a very little tragedy as mine surely needed a very little miracle to make it a comedy of errors.

Sarah came in to play, all rosy from her nap. She yawned like a very round kitten about to wash its face of cream.

"Shall we work on the doll's house?" she asked.

"No."

"Shall we sing?"

"No."

"Will you teach me a poem?"

"Yes. I will recite a poem my mother taught me. 'What is the matter with Mary Jane? What is the matter with Mary Jane?' " I began to cry.

"It's just lovely rice pudding for dinner again," said Sarah. She looked at me with her round eyes of childish disapproval. "You're crying again."

"Yes, I seem to be. It's all ended in tears."

"You need a nap." Sarah was becoming wise.

"Yes," I said, "sleep is the sovereign soporific."

I left Sarah with her nurse and I went away to take a nap.

I slept and I slept and I dreamed that a gingerbread man was running and running in the sky. An airplane came and overtook him and swallowed him up. The plane flew faster and faster toward the sun and then behind my closed eyes of sleep I saw the plane burst into flames. The accident was complete. The flames were absolute. There could be no survivors. I ran and ran trying to find Stanley and drag him from the wreckage. I could not get near the plane, it had fallen to the ground. It was surrounded by glass. The glass had turned red-hot. I burnt my hands badly trying to break the glass. It was hot, so hot, so hot. I woke up in rivers of sweat. I called Stanley in Asia Minor.

"Are you all right, Stanley?"

"Of course; very busy here. What did you want?"

"Nothing. I'm sorry, I'm sorry, I'm sorry." I hung up the phone. I looked at my hands. They were red. I had done something or left something undone, something terrible, and I had been badly burned for it. And yet, who can say, I might have gone on, same song second verse, if Simon had not come back.

28

SIMON sent a cable. "Expedition over. Coming home."
I tried to get myself pulled together but I did not think even a solid month in the ever-loving arms of Elizabeth Arden would fool Simon.

He came in September, the year Sarah was three. I went up to the gate to meet him. He'd been driven out to the Tarrytown estate in a hired Rolls which was parked self-consciously beyond the gates.

We stood on the gravel path squinting into each other's faces in the sunlight. Simon was swallowing a great deal, his Adam's apple bobbing away. He had grown a beard, like Jesus in Gethsemane, Jesus before the episode of the Cross and no cup left to drink but one. I had a tic first under my right eye, then under my left. It went on and off like a little signal of distress. Dot, dot, dash, dash.

I could not speak. I felt I was slowly strangling on a scream. We stood for a long time crunching gravel underfoot.

"You've been comforting yourself with apples," Simon said at last. "You'll get fat."

"I won't be fat." I tried to play the gay chatelaine but flunked it badly. "I'll only be plump, pleasingly plump." Simon shook his head.

"You can disappear in fat if you really want to hide. It's the greatest disappearing act of the adult Homo sapiens."

"Well," I said, "as long as I don't stay me with flagons. Apples are much more socially acceptable than flagons."

"Are you then?" Simon asked quickly.

"Am I then what?"

"Sick of love?"

"Don't be a Nosy Parker. Don't break and enter. You have no search warrant."

"What shall I be then if not the police?"

"Be my guest," I implored putting my hand on his arm.

"Guest it is," Simon looked at my hand but did not touch it. "Show me the manor, the demesne." We walked down the path from the gatehouse to the lodge. Simon gasped. "My God, it's Mayerling. Do you have Rudolph and Vetsera in a wax tableau?"

"Nothing so grand, but I've got a baby here somewhere. Do you want to see it?"

"Your issue?"

"My offspring."

"Your sprout?"

"My sprig."

"Is it viewable?"

"Oh, yes," I said. "Nap-nap time is over. It's mother's playtime now. Ignore the nurse. She's fierce. She's had both infants and seniles and finds it best to treat relatives as if they were both."

"Is the 'it' still in its pram?"

"Lord, no, it's on the hoof. It's peripatetic."

"I'm ever so sorry, I'm sure," Simon said, mock solemn.

"You must remember," I chided, "one in every three children is peripatetic."

Simon laughed. I had made a little joke and Simon had laughed. Out came the nurse with Sarah. We stood in the clouded amber of autumn and watched Sarah tottering and reeling about the lawn.

"Your baby is drunk," Simon said at last.

"Oh, what a thing to say," bridled Nursey.

"Lovely Nursey, do go and have a nice cup of tea."

"Well then," said lovely Nursey, setting her mouth for tea and reprimand, "but mind, you take good care of Baby."

Simon and I watched Sarah gambol in and out of the hedge. She was plump and pleasing. There had been neither apples nor flagons for her, just lots and lots of orange juice out of frosted silver cups. Sarah smiled up at us, a mouth full of perfect teeth like an add-a-pearl necklace, a suitable string of presents for every occasion. She was a pretty thing.

"I must know," Simon asked softly, "was the escape committee a success? Did you break the sound barrier? Have you landed on the moon? Did Conway get back to Shangri-La? Is Margo still young? Are the bluebirds of happiness still flying?"

"Stop it. Stop it," I cried, savage that he should ask.

"I came all this way to find the answer," Simon persisted. I could not look at him, I only saw Sarah.

"If you must hear it, Simon, the answer is no. My adjustment to bliss has been very poor."

"I'm sorry," Simon said.

"Are you?" There was the scream in the throat again. I had to push the words around it to get them out.

"Yes," Simon was watching me, "I am sorry."

"What else?"

"Forbearing."

"You don't have to forbear, Simon, you can say 'I told you so' if you want to."

"I don't."

"You can even laugh like the gods if you like."

"I don't like."

"Well," I sighed. The baby and the grass all blurred together. "The gods aren't laughing either. The joke's too old."

I was afraid Simon was going to take me in his arms and

pat me. I shied away. I couldn't have comfort. Even one pat would be fatal. If Simon was kind to me I'd cry for a hundred years.

"What are you going to do now?" he asked.

"Nothing."

"That's not like you."

"I know. I'm not like me at all."

"What does the husband say?"

"Nothing."

"Why, for God's sake?"

"First rule of the Partridge family is, don't stir the pot. If you stir, something rude and unattractive may float to the top."

"Suppose it does?"

"Deny everything! We lead the unexamined life here. That's civilization. Didn't you know? The pot must be kept bubbling at all costs. The fire must never go out. In this life there are all the newts and toads this old world has got to offer. Just make the best of the stew. Be a steward over it. Tend it well and in time pass it along to the next generation."

"And what about the 'it'?" Simon demanded. "Do you want her to inherit the pot passed on, mother to daughter?"

"I don't know, Simon, she might like an old unstirred pot. I don't know her terribly well. We're rather like the only two English-speaking passengers on a stalled Siberian railway. We nod but we can't speak because we've never been properly introduced."

There was a big hole of silence. I thought to close the gap.

"So what's new by you, Simon?"

"Sidney's dead."

"Oh, I'm sorry. I didn't know."

"He left a fortune. One for me and one for Shirl. She

wants me to run the business and bring out the fall line. She says we could call it Ethiopian Eye Openers."

"You won't, will you Simon? You'll go back to your work."

"What work?"

"Your scrolls. How are your scrolls?"

"Wet," Simon said. "They built their dam and flooded the valley of the caves." Now it was my turn to look at Simon who could not look at me.

"I'm sorry, Simon."

"Are you?"

"Yes."

"It didn't really matter," Simon said, kicking at the grass with the heel of his shoe. "I'd managed to translate most of them."

"That's marvelous." Simon gave a great jab with his heel.

"A marvelous fool, that's me. They turned out to be bills of lading for camel caravans. No revelation, no holy writ, no message of love after all, just a long accounting of the gelt of days gone by. If there was a Messiah he came and was killed and if he came again he was killed again. The same story over and over." Simon tried to tamp the grass back into place but it was hopeless. He gave it up and looked at me.

"What are you going to do, Simon?"

"Go to Paris. Sidney always said everyone should see Paris before they die."

"Oh Simon, eat lots of lovely Béarnaise sauce for me."

"Come with me."

"To Paris?"

"Yes. Eat your own sauce."

I was overcome. The eyes went back and forth, ticcing away like crazy. I looked at Sarah chasing after a butterfly.

"Can I bring the future of the nation?"

"If you want to. I'd always take care of the 'it.'"

"Love me, love my child." Simon blinked and in the blink

of an eye I saw Paris vanish. "That was unfair, Simon. I'm sorry."

"I don't promise to love you as you want to be loved but I want you to come. Both of you." Simon would never change and neither would I.

"Why? I can be unloved at home."

"I can take care of you and I'll take care of Sarah."

"We have very high-class custodial care here."

"Mine would be better." Simon was pleading.

"I don't see how. If there's to be no love, then what can you offer?"

"I'd buy the 'it' lots of little white gloves and I'd let her eat marrons glacés in the Madeleine."

"It would make her sick and the gloves would get dirty."

"Tell me what you want, then."

"Besides love?"

"Yes, besides that."

"Nothing."

"We could do useful work. We could buy an electric organ and go out and join Schweitzer."

"And Sarah? What would Sarah do in the jungle?"

"A medical missionary for the children."

"No, Simon. Thanks, but no thanks." Simon was defeated and he knew it. "I cannot go, Simon," I said. "It would be like Helen bolting from all her great loves that did not work out. I cannot take Sarah from Stanley. It would be my life story over again for her."

"If you need me," Simon said, "or Sarah, if either of you need me I'm available. You have only to ask."

"What will you do in Paris when you aren't eating my Béarnaise sauce?"

"Why," Simon managed a smile, "I'll run down to American Express for the remittance checks and I'll wait for your call."

"You'll have the gelt."

"Do you need any? You have only to ask."

"No Simon, I'm all right."

"Have you thought of going back to work? I always said the stage was much the best for you."

"If I had a theatre of my own I'd act."

"Yes, Virginia," said Simon, "there is a Woolf."

I laughed and Simon laughed and neither wanted to be the first to stop.

"What's left to say?" I asked Simon.

"What can I say, dear, after I've said I'm sorry," and he patted me.

I started to cry most unreasonably, great big sobs the size of tennis balls bobbed up around the scream that would not dissolve. Sarah looked up startled and saw the two adults, one sobbing, the other stamping holes in the grass. She ran off to find her keeper.

Simon put his arms around me and held me tight while I sobbed and wailed like a creature from another planet.

"Oh, Simon, oh, Simon, if I had been better and worked harder, I could have made you love me."

"Oh, don't you believe it, honey dear. There was no way, no how. You've got no guilt to carry for me."

I must have been making a hideous noise. Lovely Nursey came charging across the green grass ready for battle.

"Here now, here now, what's all this?" she bellowed at Simon. "What have you done to Mummy?"

"I've dealt her a lifetime blow," said Simon and he kissed me and he went away.

29

S TILL, I might have gone on year in and year out feeling it
was my duty to put one foot in front of the other down
the straight and narrow path of the death in life if it had
not been for the scandal in Asia Minor.

It was on the front page of the *New York Times*. Stanley
was accused of failing to properly administer some warehouses full of rice. I came down to breakfast and sat with my
orange juice and coffee just as I had sat in that house of his
mother's every day at breakfast. I opened the *Times* and
there on the front page was a picture of Stanley and head-
lines of such horror that they twisted like snakes. I think I
made some sound. I must have, for Nursey came in from
another room and asked me what was the matter.

"Nothing," I said, "there is ice in the orange juice and it
surprised me. I'm not used to ice in orange juice. It hurt my
teeth."

"Oh," said Nursey. She gave me a look of disapproval.
"Well, drink it anyway, it's good for you," and she left.

I had folded the paper so she would not see Stanley's
picture. It was foolish. I knew it was foolish when I did it
because the truth was bound to come out. It was out now in
every edition. I drank my coffee scalding hot and then I
made myself open the paper and read the news.

There was a war being fought in Asia Minor; a delaying

action, the paper called it. Both sides refused to feed the people because they could not come to an agreement as to who had the right to the rice in the government granaries. Now there was a time of famine. The people must be fed or starve to death. Even governments cannot have a war without people. So the Partridge Foundation had been called in to dole out the supply fairly to both sides. Stanley had been made responsible for the warehouses. The responsibility was his. He was the person in authority. When the warehouses were opened there was no rice there, no rice at all. Now Stanley stood charged with having sold the rice for his own profit or having turned a Nelson eye while the rice was taken. I could not make out all the charges, they were so carefully worded in *Times* language. It was alleged that he had done something and there was to be an inquiry.

I was shaking with fear and terror because there must be something wrong with me or I would have known Stanley was in danger. I would have been able to reach out and help him. It was my dream, my nightmare come true. I looked at the paper again. The words blurred and refocused. Stanley, the paper said, was returning on an afternoon plane.

I went to the airport to meet him. The flight was delayed. I walked up and down the terminal in more terror, fearful that the rest of the dream might come true and that the plane might crash and I would never be able to get to him at all. It was like being in a hospital corridor waiting for the end of the operation.

At last his plane arrived. I watched for him through the glass visitors' enclosure. He was almost the last passenger on his flight to come into the customs area. He did not even look up to see if I was there. He was so worn and so thin, his face so twisted with pain that I felt the knife from his wounds in my heart.

After he went through the routine inspection two men came and escorted him into a room marked Press. I found the room from another corridor and went inside. It was full of working reporters and photographers all asking questions and flashing lightbulbs. The room was hot and smoke-filled. Where, I wondered, did they find all the smoke for smoke-filled rooms. Surely human lungs could not manufacture it all.

Watching Stanley be so besieged was horror. They were breaking every bone in his body. He was as bedeviled as a mediaeval man in the miracle plays. I ached. Still he did not see me. At the last of the inquisition, when they had had their fill of his blood and his flesh, the press conference was over. There was a dwindling away, only the stale smoke remained like the last falling ash of martyrs' fires. Stanley was standing, his back to me, talking to some men from the Foundation.

"Stanley," I said. He turned and looked at me as if I were a ghost, as Brandon had looked at me as he came off the stage with his stage child. "I'm here, I've come to take you home."

"I can't come home," he said, "I've got to go to the office and work on a report. I have to gather the figures for the inquiry. They start sitting tomorrow." I might as well have been a lady reporter come late for an official story.

"Come home just for tonight."

"No, I can't do that, not now."

"Please." I was begging like a little dog for scraps. I would have barked or lain at his feet. "Please, can't we go someplace where we can talk?" He shook his head as if to reset his brain. He had been on that plane a long time and he was tired.

"Yes," he said slowly and distinctly, "yes, we'll talk. We'd better do that." He spoke to the Partridge men for a moment and then we went out into the airport lobby.

"Where shall we go?" I asked, trying to fall into his step.

He was walking very fast. Was he trying to escape from me or himself?

"I know," he said. He put two dimes into a gate marked Observation Terrace.

We went out onto the deck. The planes were everywhere. The air was filled with the roar of the jets coming in and taking off. It made communication difficult. There was so much noise that we could not hear each other's thinking. We were forced to shout at each other as if we were having an argument.

"Are you all right?" I asked into the wind and the noise. What a silly question when he was so very obviously so very far from all right.

"I've not absconded with the rice, if that's what you want to know." I had not attacked but he was on the defensive, his reflexes were still set for battle.

"No," I said, "that's not what I wanted to know. That's not what I mean. I wanted to know if you were all right."

"Yes," he said, sagging a bit, putting down his shield. "I'm tired but I'm all right. This is all one big mess. They've got to find someone to blame and my name is on the door. But don't worry, it's going to be all right."

"I'm not worried about that, I'm worried about you. Please let me take you home and tend you."

"I can't do that," Stanley said, "I'm running late now. I've got to get a whole mass of correspondence from the office and start to plow through it little by little. Try to justify figures and facts."

"But where will you sleep? Where will you rest your head?"

"Oh, that," Stanley paused and thought. "I'm going to my mother's."

"To your mother's?" I was going to have to have that repeated.

"Well, not to her apartment, but to her building. She's

taken an apartment for me there, it's all arranged. There'll be no one to disturb me."

"And she's arranged it all?"

"Yes." Stanley looked relieved of a burden. "She's being just wonderful about all this. She sent a cable." He fumbled in a coat pocket. "Here, let me read it to you. She says, 'We'll fight this through together and win.' "

"She's a formidable lady, your mother."

"Yes, isn't she?" Stanley was ever sincere, never more so than now. He put the cable back in his pocket. "She's sent a car to meet me to bring me into town."

"Your mother," I said, "is driving and she's in perfect control." Stanley's brow furrowed.

"No, she can't drive, she's sent a hired limousine." I sighed, the wind went out of me.

"Listen," I said, trying not to shout and yet be heard, "this is a crisis you're having, isn't it?"

"Yes," Stanley said slowly.

"A real-life genuine crisis?"

"Yes."

"Then," I said, trying not to cry and trying very hard to keep in one piece and not go shattering off into childish attitudes, "I think we ought to be together. I think we ought to cleave together like crazy."

"Diana, I'm fighting for my life, my business life, can't you see that?"

"Yes, but what's that got to do with staying together?"

"I'll come home when I can. This is a business that you don't know and my mother does. She's pretty remarkable to understand so well what I'm up against."

"If I'm your loved one now is the time for holding close."

"I haven't got time for holding close. I'm beset. I don't want to sound paranoid but I think the world is against me today." I put my arms around him and held him as tight as ever I could. I was needing him so much that I thought surely he must be needing me as much in return.

"Please," I said, "just come home and let me feed you dinner, pack you a suitcase with clean shirts and socks and underwear. Then you can go. I won't run after you."

"Does it mean so much?"

"Yes, I'm asking most humbly." He kissed me lightly on the top of the head.

"If you let me look at my watch I'll see how much time there is." I let him go. He looked at his watch. "It's after three," he said, "if we go now we could have dinner and then I could go in town but by the time I got there the evening would be shot. I'd like to come, Diana, you know that."

"Oh, I hope so." There was a long pause.

"I can't," he said, "I really can't. My mother's got some old friends from the Foundation coming after dinner. They are in a position to know what's going on from the inside. I must go, you see that. My mother's waiting."

"I see that," I said, "indeed I do. Shall I send the socks and things anyway?"

"Yes, that's a good idea, you do that."

"I will."

"I'll call you to tell you my suite number."

"Yes, do, but then I can get that from the desk clerk, can't I?"

"Yes, you can. You know the number."

"Yes."

"I think we ought to go in now," he said, "it's turning cold."

"I'm freezing to death," I said.

"September can be a treacherous month. You should have brought a coat."

"Yes, I never know what to wear. I always choose the wrong thing. I never know when it's going to turn cold." We went back into the airport and he kissed me goodbye as absently as if I were putting him on the morning train and he'd be home by nightfall.

I felt I had been hit in the face with the Partridge fist. The blood was salty in my mouth and the teeth were loose. I felt savage to be sent on my way, dismissed when I wanted, if not to be needed, at least to be wanted. I had been playing a very long game in the land of the Partridge, a game called, "Choose me, choose me," and I had always been odd man out of the three of us. For a little scrap of hope that I'd be chosen loved one of the year, child of the heart, I had been running round and round the rugged rock and I was ragged.

I went away home because Sarah was there and surely she needed me. As I was going up to the house she met me on the gravel path. She had been waiting for me, I had not had much time for her this day. She came up and put her arms around my knees.

How clumsy children are when they are looking for love. Her hands were sticky from her teatime bread and jam. They left their imprint on my clean, tidy going-out-into-the-world clothes. It was an indelible ink of need that would not rub off or wash off and could never be gotten rid of at the cleaners.

"Play with me," Sarah said.

"Not now, I have a pain." She clung to my legs.

"I want you to play with me."

"Let me go, Sarah," I tried to pry her away from me. Children are so very strong.

"No."

"Let me go."

"No, no, no."

In a rage at not being able to answer her need, I gave her the back of my hand. I knocked her down. She sat on the gravel path, scratched and beginning to bleed, her face bewildered, pained, incredulous. Then she saw the blood and began to whimper and to cry in great, bereaved wails of utter anguish.

What did I do? What did I do? Too late I took her in my arms. I rocked her back and forth savagely, trying to make her stop, trying to undo the damage and the harm I had done her.

"I love you, Sarah, don't cry. I know you don't believe I love you but I do." I heard myself say it then, Brandon's own words to me. I was giving her my legacy all over again. I had been hit and so I had hit out and I had hit Sarah.

Lovely Nursey had watched the scene and stood waiting for her cue. She stepped forward, arms outstretched.

"What have you done to the child?" she demanded.

"I have dealt her a lifetime blow," I said and I handed her Sarah and I ran and I ran, the knowledge of what I had said to Sarah hounding after me like the black and angry ones. I must run and run until I could find me a sacred grove where I could lie down and sleep. I must look for a temple where Artemis would ring me round with protecting trees and guard my image as I might guard hers. Had Artemis not been the goddess of childbed, another name for Diana? I felt that I had been both the violated and now the violator of all life given in trust to me.

I ran until I came to a taxi. I directed the driver to take me to Helen's madhouse as quickly as possible. I had been avoiding Helen in her exile, I had stopped seeing her. I had stopped even limited communication. I was afraid to ask her anything, even the time of the year, because she was sure to tell me that eleven o'clock would come or to ask me for scraps that I could not find it in my heart to send.

But I needed her and so I went to her. We had a distant meeting on the evening veranda. We sat in wicker chairs taking the evening view of all the promenading inmates, pathetic dropouts from the lifetime struggle, not really mad, just out-of-bounds souls who had never been able to follow directions of their own or anyone else's and had ended up arrested for getting off the path and onto the grass once too often. I began at once. I had no time to waste.

"Helen," I asked, "why did you leave the husband in Ham?" Helen looked totally startled as if she did not know to whom I might refer.

"Oh," she said, sudden recollection in her voice, "him."

"Yes," I said, "him."

"Oh," she said, making a rue face, "I had to leave. Ham and him, because both he and the Ham were too dreary to bear."

"And the boys?" I pursued her. "Were they dreary, too?"

"No, dear," she smiled softly as if she knew a secret, "they weren't dreary, they just weren't mine."

"How's that again?" Now it was my turn to be startled.

"I mean," she said, "that they were like him."

"Oh," I said, "yes," not understanding at all.

"Children are like one or they are not, don't you know? Just because they are blood and bone doesn't make them yours."

"Oh."

"You don't see, but you will."

"Will I?"

"Yes, but don't worry, she'll be like you. Your child, what's her name again?"

"Sarah."

"Sarah will be like you." I was confounded. This was not the Helen I had expected nor the answer I had thought to get.

"She looks like Brandon," I said, bewildered.

"Yes, I saw that in the photograph you sent."

"She's not like me," I said. "She's got masses of black hair and red, red lips and she cries a lot."

"She'll be like you." Helen was confident.

"I cry a lot. I don't want her to be like me."

Helen looked at me sharply. "I don't remember Brandon crying."

"He cries all the time," I said.

"Brandon?" Helen was blue-eyed disbelief.

"Yes."

"Isn't that odd? I never saw Brandon crying."

"Well, he does." I went at Helen again. "Why did you leave Brandon?"

"Oh dear," Helen said, "a visitation of questions."

"Yes," I said, "answers please. Helen, I'm saying please. I want to know why you left. I thought he was the love of your life."

"He was." Helen was definite.

"You said I was the fruit of that great love."

"You were."

"And yet you left him."

"Or he left me," Helen said. "I really don't remember now who left whom. I mean who walked out and slammed the door. I've always said that I walked out of the house but I think it was Brandon. Yes, it was Brandon now that I think of it. He slammed the door on Nora."

"What?"

"Nora," Helen said, "in *A Doll's House*. Don't you remember Ibsen's door-slam heard round the world? Don't you know any plays?"

"Stick to the subject," I said. "Why did you leave each other? You can share the billing for once, there's a dear, do. Why did you both leave me?"

"Well Brandon got dreary, too dreary to bear."

"Like the chemist?"

"No, not like the chemist."

"But dreary."

"Yes, very dreary, weary."

"Define dreary, Helen." Helen was a long time in silent thought. Finally she sighed and spoke.

"Wanting me to be the same, you know. Now there's the truth."

"No, I don't know. You'll have to be very articulate with me. I'm dumb, I'm your idiot child." Helen thought again.

"I mind having to be faithful. I can't be the constant wife and it's no good my trying."

"You mean men and all that?" I said, trying to face some reality in my inexplicable mum.

"Lord no," Helen said, "not men at all. It's a matter of identity. People fall in love with me because they see me in a certain way and then they want me to be that way no matter how I really am. It makes them cross if I change the way I do my hair. I can't be the same day in and day out and so I end up being a disappointment and I'm disapproved of and I have to leave because it's all too dreary."

"Don't they change too? Is it always just you?"

"I don't know," Helen said, "I don't notice other people much, I only notice me."

I was speechless.

"I'm an actress," Helen said. "I don't have to notice the audience more than to count up and see that they are there. They have to notice me. It's my job to act, to play the parts, to get the applause. If I have to stay the same in the same house with the same people it's too much like being at home again, like being someone's child."

"It must have all been so dreary when you were a child," I said. I had a sudden flood of affection for Helen. "I should have told you before, I met your dear old mum when I was in merry old England."

"Did you?" Helen swallowed and her mouth twisted.

"Helen, why did you tell me that your mum was lovely and ladylike and smelled of lavender?"

"Because I couldn't say my mum was ugly and tatty and smelled of gin."

"You still send her two pound ten a week."

"Who?"

"Your mum."

"Not my mum. I have no mum. Nothing that can be bought for two pound ten a week is worthy to be my mum." I had a lump in my throat for Helen.

"Mr. Margolies loves you a lot, doesn't he?"

"Yes," Helen said, "my, yes. He's the best audience I ever had. He'll let me play any part I choose, although he likes it best when I play Helen Shell the greatest actress of her time. That's why I stay on here, you know."

"What?" My turn for twitching.

"Oh yes," Helen said, "when the play failed I couldn't bear to see Eric so unhappy. I had to come here. I had failed before his very eyes. It nearly killed him. I had to come here. Here I can be a living legend. He can keep my scrapbooks and the illusion of me as his own special divinity. I'm very fond of Eric. I don't want to see him hurt. The only thing he ever did in his whole life that he was proud of was to marry me. I can't become a nobody, a failure. Think of what that would do to him. At least here I can preserve his illusion that I was the greatest actress of my time, struck down by madness in my zenith. He won't have to face up to the reality that I wore myself out appearing like a fool in a foolish play when I was past my prime." I had a sudden burning to give Helen an enormous cup of comfort.

"You were very good in the play," I said. "It was the play that was no good. It was a lousy script."

"I was a dated back number," said Helen, "but thanks for the good and kind notice. That's the nicest thing you could possibly do for your dear old mum."

"I always thought you were here because I was mean and pushed you over the edge." Helen gasped.

"You thought you drove me here?"

"Yes."

"Well, what a laugh." Helen was appalled. "You do yourself too much honor."

"I see that," I said, "but that's one of my illusions, guilt. It was my balloon of gas and wind and now it's all gone bust."

"Sorry to cost you your illusion, but you did ask the questions. Well, keep your illusions if you can, they carry you away from places you don't like to be."

"Illusion can't keep the Emperor warm."

"What?"

"Don't you know any children's stories?" I was peevish. " 'The Emperor's New Clothes.' He thought he was in robes of gold and he was naked."

"I suppose you have some illusion that you are going to jump your tight little domestic ship because it's all gotten to be too dreary."

"Think again. I want us to stay afloat, all of us: captain, first mate and crew, I just don't know how to manage it. I'm in a present terror because it has occurred to me that if I'm going to treat Sarah the way you treated me I might as well move in with you now. It would save a lot of useless misery all around."

"That's impossible. You don't belong here. Even Eric has to live off the grounds. Besides you're not like me and that child of yours is not you."

"I think I'm naked in a patterned dumb show and the pattern is coming full circle."

"Well, it's not."

"Why not, Helen, prove it. Give me one of your words of wisdom now."

"I'll tell you why not. I'm selfish, I think of me. You don't have any talent for self."

"I always thought I was very selfish."

"Illusion again. You don't think enough of yourself to keep you warm in winter."

"You are crazy or I am."

"Not at all." Helen was firm. "You've always been like that. When you were a child we'd go out to the park and even on the coldest days you wouldn't take a coat. You'd just stand there all blue and goose bumps and you'd begin to whine and jump up and down first on one leg and then the other. Well, I'll say to you now what wisdom I said to you then, 'If you don't care enough for yourself to wear a coat when it's cold, it's no good moaning, Monica.'" I was suddenly wild with Helen.

"That's just a line, a line from some play you were in, my name's Diana, not Monica." Helen drew herself high and haughty.

"Just because I said it in a play doesn't mean it's not true or that I didn't say it to you."

"All right, Helen, all right." I sought to mollify and smooth her feelings. "I've asked the questions and you've given me your answers. You can't say fairer than that."

"Shall we kiss each other goodbye?" Helen asked. "It's getting dark, it's the end of visiting hours."

"Yes let's," I said. We kissed, and in our own way I think we made it up between us.

30

IT had never occurred to me that I was not thinking of
self day and night, that I might not be the most selfish
girl in the world. I had always had a terrible feeling that I
was selfish, selfish, selfish, mean and ugly. Well, now that
was something to think over, like a bucket of cold water in
the face.

Even I noticed that this night was chill. I had noticed the
change in weather in the afternoon at the airport. Perhaps I
was capable of learning a thing or two yet. I did know that
the only overcoat I wished to bespeak me was Stanley's open
arms, and they were in another place. If he was what I
wanted, why not be selfish? Why be all three of the three
sillies about his coming home. If he could not come to me I
could go to him. If it were the other way around and I were
harried and beset and hounded, I would expect Stanley to
come to me, so why should I not rally round his frayed and
tattered standard?

If he could not serve me I could serve him. He had been
there for me on a night when I had needed him, was it not
seemly and ladylike of me to be there when he needed me? I
counted the blessing of Lovely Nursey who could hold the
fort in Tarrytown and guard Sarah until I could get back to
make amends to her.

It was true that I did not have a suitcase full of clean

laundry with me, but surely I would not be any the less welcome for that. Laundry could wait until tomorrow. Tonight I could get the Brasserie to put up a picnic basket or stop at a delicatessen. I would call Stanley and see what he had been longing to eat and then I would not come empty-handed or unlooked-for.

While he shuffled his papers I could make pots of coffee and when he had finished I could rub his neck or tell him stories until he fell asleep. I could be of endless good cheer. I had cried so many tears in the past that being a dry-eyed brick might some way partly make it up to him. It was stupid of me not to have thought of it before. It was such an eminently sensible plan.

I had the easiest possible time finding the telephone number for the apartment house. Yes, they did indeed have a Mr. Partridge and they would put me through at once. The telephone began to ring. In a moment Stanley would answer and it would be all right. The receiver came off the hook. I was the first to speak.

"Hello, Stanley. Hello," I said again.

"Hello," it was a woman's voice. My first thought was that they had given me the wrong number and my second thought a blackout line from an old review sketch. "If a woman answers, hang up." I wish I had. "Hello," the woman's voice said again. It was Mrs. Partridge.

"Hello, this is Diana. Is Stanley there?"

"Diana, no dear, he's downstairs in my apartment in a meeting."

"Oh."

"I just had my key in the door when I heard the phone ring."

"Oh." There was a rustling of paper, a radio sound effect of burning buildings. "Well," I said, "I'm on my way over and I thought there might be something he wanted, something he needed." More crumpling paper.

"That's very thoughtful of you, Diana, but I've seen to all that. I think I've got everything here that he could possibly need."

"Oh." I wished I'd stop saying, oh. Another pause and a thump.

"Diana."

"Yes." Now there was something besides oh; not brilliant but different.

"Is Stanley expecting you?"

"No."

"Oh." Now it was her turn. "Well then, Diana, may I be frank?" Be Frank. Be George. Be Fred if you like, I thought wildly, only be quick.

"Of course," I said quite nicely.

"Well then, I don't think your coming here would be a good idea."

"Why not?"

"Surely," Mrs. Partridge was being most patient, "you must know how serious this whole affair is."

"I think so."

"And how upset Stanley is by it."

"I went to the airport. I saw him, he looks awful."

"He said you had been out there." So they had discussed me. "He said that you had gone home."

"I had," I said, "I went home good as gold."

"What?"

"I went home but I left again."

"Diana."

"Yes."

"This meeting tonight is going to take I don't know how long. Then there's tomorrow to fight through. I've come up to unpack for him and to make him as comfortable as possible under the circumstances." She sounded like the floor nurse in a distant hospital.

"I think," I said, "I'd feel better there than at home."

217

"But it's Stanley we must think about, isn't it?" Oh, how badly I was doing this.

"It is Stanley I'm thinking about, I think."

"He's going to need as much rest as possible."

"I'll be very quiet and good," I said. "I'm really very useful."

"Please, Diana, don't be dramatic. This is not a play."

"I didn't mean to be dramatic, I meant to be cheerful."

"I'm sorry. Yes, of course you are, but you do see this is a terrific strain on him."

"Yes, I see that."

"And if you want to be a real help . . ."

"I do."

"I think you should go on back to Tarrytown."

"Why?"

"You can be the very best use to him by taking care of Sarah."

"Lovely Nursey is there."

"Diana, in the Partridge family we have always tried to take care of our own. I'll take care of Stanley and you take care of my granddaughter. You can do that for now and later when he's able, when we've got this mistake made right, then I know he'll want to see you."

"You don't think he wants to see me now, is that it?"

"You must not misunderstand me, Diana."

"I'm trying not to."

"Stanley is at the breaking point. One more added consideration and he could be very ill." Mrs. Partridge was no longer Stanley's nurse; now she was his doctor. "I don't want to alarm you, but when I saw him I knew what had to be done." How formidable to be able to diagnose and prescribe remedies in an instant. "I've made arrangements for him to see a psychiatrist."

"Stanley?" I could not believe that he was really that badly off. Stanley was tired and in a bind but Stanley was the steadiest and strongest person I had ever known. There wasn't any flaw in him that needed mending. "Has something happened? Something you're not telling me?"

"No, Diana, it was my decision to call a doctor. I'd be a poor mother if I did not do what I know to be right for Stanley." I was defeated by that. I wished I knew the absolute difference between right and wrong. Perhaps then I'd be a proper mother. "I've arranged for him to see Dr. Glass. He's the most eminent man in his field."

"Dr. Glass." He was spoken of highly. Even I knew that much. Mrs. Partridge would never have called in an ordinary run of the track workman for Stanley.

"And Stanley has agreed to see him?" I wondered.

"Certainly." Mrs. Partridge was the brick and I the reed in the wind. "Please leave this to me. I'll be in touch if there's anything you can do."

"Thank you, Mrs. Partridge." Once again she had given me an unasked-for and unwelcome gift and all I could say was thank you.

"You'll go home now?"

"Yes."

"And take care of Sarah?"

"Yes."

"And let Dr. Glass and me take care of Stanley?"

"Yes, and let you and Dr. Glass take care of Stanley."

And I did as I was told, good as gold.

31

But the gold left a green mark on me. It was Woolworth's and not Tiffany's. In the alchemy of my mind Mrs. Partridge's philosopher's stone would make no treasure for me. I tried to see it the way it was presented through Mrs. Partridge's spectacles. I saw nothing to keep me warm or comfort me.

I had Sarah and she forgave me my blow as children do without holding a grudge. She made up a story for me to cover my bad behavior, one that would content her.

"You must have had a tummyache," she said when I said I was sorry. "You must have eaten green apples."

"Perhaps," I said. "Perhaps that's it."

"Yes," Sarah said, and she told it that way just to set herself straight. I heard her tell Nursey. "When my mother hit me it was because she had eaten a lot of green apples and she had a terrible pain in her tummy." Nursey shook her head silently and pricked at my conscience by asking every day, "Is your tummyache all right now?" And I'd say, "Yes." It got to be a morning ritual, the green-apple address, and then I'd take my coffee into the morning room, for it was too windy and cold for the garden in the morning, and I'd read about Stanley.

The inquiry went to the back pages very soon and I had to hunt for the story. Mrs. Partridge called from time to time and Stanley too, but neither of them said more than I could have read in the paper.

Mrs. Partridge went with him every day to the inquiry. It was a family affair and seemingly there was no way for me ever to become a member of the clan. I sent in the laundry. It was my bit, my little Care parcel. Although I meant not to brood or dwell or be morbid I found sleep a sometime thing and peace of mind an impossible.

If I could get nothing from the nurse or the patient, why not ask the doctor? I called to make an appointment to see Dr. Glass. He would be more than happy to talk with me at my convenience.

I do not know what I had expected of him. I think I had a fantasy of a beard and a pipe. There was no beard and no pipe.

"Won't you sit down?" he asked me. Had I expected him to ask me to lie down upon his couch? I sat down and I looked at Dr. Glass, to whom Stanley talked when he could not talk to me, and Dr. Glass looked at me and I wondered what he saw; and suddenly, for no reason at all, I heard me say, "Help." What a strange thing to say.

"How can I help you?"

"I don't know. I feel like I'm back at school and sitting for the French exam. It's too hard for me. I can't read the questions, let alone answer them. I think I've done something absolutely dreadful and I don't know what it is and no one will tell me. You know, I've got bad breath or diseased armpits or worse."

"Why do you think that?" he smiled.

"Stanley," I said, "he's gone in a crash and I can't reach him. It's not funny," I said, "wait till you hear my life story. It's nothing to smile about. People can't wait to leave me or have me leave them. I must have done something. I mean mother, father, friend and foe alike. Can you tell me if I'm mad? I feel mad."

"Angry perhaps."

"A rage," I said, "not anger. Anger is a little word. I've got a rage like a terrible tiger. I'm in a nightmare and I want it to stop. I've done something awful to Stanley or he wouldn't be coming to you and living with his mother."

"Tell me the nightmare."

"Where to begin?"

"At the beginning."

I began with Helen and Brandon and me in the middle.

"Have you any idea," I said, "how exhausting it is to be parent to your parents? It takes it out of you. I'm still tired from it. I sleep a lot." I told about Mr. Margolies and how he tended me instead of my tending him, about learning to act and Simon tending me as best as he was able. About Helen going mad after her fashion, about the jolly lecher and the penance and the pilgrimage, about the Iphigenia and Stanley, about finding my true love and living in his mother's house and never having anything of my own except Sarah and how I was afraid I'd made a botch of motherhood and wifehood and just plain peoplehood; most of all being afraid I had somehow been responsible for wounding Stanley.

"Oh dear," I said, "that's about the lot. I can't think of anything else to tell you. You see I must change my tiger stripes or perish. That is if it isn't too late, if I haven't already eaten Stanley."

"Eaten him alive?"

"Yes, like the gingerbread man. Do you know the story?"

"Yes." He smiled again.

"I wish you'd stop smiling."

"Why?"

"I've always felt simpleminded. I think you're laughing at me. I may not have very big problems but they're mine."

"Do you cling to them?"

"Sometimes they're my portrait, the picture of me."

"You do realize," Dr. Glass stopped smiling and started

looking terribly like a doctor, "that Stanley's problem is not you at all, it's his mother." I gasped.

"Why would you tell me a thing like that?"

"Because it's true."

"Stanley has a very big mother," I said. "She's as large as her shadow, but you can't know Stanley very well. He's able to slay dragons and move mountains and still have half a day left over."

"Is that how you see him?"

"That's how he is. He came and rescued me. I was a damsel in distress. That makes him a white knight, doesn't it?"

"No."

"It's cruel to joke with me. I told you I wasn't too bright."

"It's very common for girls whose fathers have left them at an early age to over-idealize the male."

"I may be a case history, Freud's own daughter and all that, but you must be wrong about Stanley."

"No, that's my professional opinion."

"Oh dear," I said, "oh dear, oh dear me."

"What's the matter?"

"You've taken my balloons," I said, "all my illusions are going one by one. It's a death in the family to lose them all. What's going to happen now? What will become of me?"

"Become of you or Stanley?"

"Of me, because if Stanley is not Stanley then I am not me any more. How can I ever be sure of anything again if I could not be sure of him. I saw him with my own eyes and there was never another like him."

"You've told yourself a lot of stories and you've been told a lot of stories. Telling the truth will be easier. There isn't anything wrong in thinking well of yourself for a change."

"Well, I can't think well of me if I don't have Stanley. Why did you have to tell me all that? Why didn't you just say it was all my fault and let me go. I'd gotten used to being

God's most impossible creature. It's really unfair of you to break my glasses and hand me yours."

"I did not hand you mine. I don't wear them. Don't put words in my mouth."

"You have to leave me something."

"What do you want to have?"

"I cannot give up one last hope."

"What is that hope?"

"Simon," I said, "I have to believe that Simon is perfect." I tore off sheet after sheet of Kleenex and blew and blew my nose.

"Tell me about Simon. How do you see Simon?"

"I see Simon very well," I said. "Simon is my buddy chum pal. We communicate he and I. He says things to me and I say things to him and Simon always laughs at my jokes."

"Always?"

"Well, almost always. Simon loves me."

"Is Simon your lover?"

"No."

"Yet you say he loves you."

"Yes, and Simon never lies."

"What else does Simon say?"

"Simon says that loving is your lifetime luggage. Simon says that you inherit your luggage from your mother and father. Simon says that growing up is learning to be responsible for your luggage. I mean you can carry it or check it or travel with it. You can try and lose it. You can pack it at the analyst's and rearrange the contents. You can send it to storage. You can hide it in the attic. You can take it to Tahiti but all the love you have is just that inherited piece of luggage. It's the gift you were given."

"And what else does Simon say?"

"Simon says that love is a heavenly parcel. Simon says that no love is a black pigskin valise full of death. Simon says that people like Mrs. Partridge make do with an old Gladstone

bag. Simon says that all Sidney and Shirley got was a brown
paper sack full of dirty pictures. Simon says that Helen and
Brandon each have a costume trunk with lots of funny hats.
Simon says my long-lost brother Roland has a lute full of
tunes without words. Simon says I've got a pocket of bogus
dreams. Simon says that I have Stanley and he has me and a
poor lot of good we have been to each other, each so busy
carrying a lot of handicap weights that don't belong to us.
And Simon says that Sarah, poor Sarah, hasn't anything at all
to carry if we don't give it to her. Poor Sarah.

"Simon says that as scarce as we have made love, some will
go mad and some will die, that saints will make martyrs of
themselves, poets will catch us in a verse and the rest must
carry what they have the best way they can, because unless a
miracle occurs there is no more love to be had."

When I had finished the good doctor thought a long time
and then he said, "Now that you have told me what Simon
says, tell me what you say."

"I say I am Simon and he is me. Only I have to go on
believing in the possibility of a miracle for Sarah if not for
me."

"What else do you say?" I thought a long time.

"I say that Simon never said any of those things, I did."

"What did Simon really say?"

"He said that it was all the guilt and the gelt. Oh dear."
Suddenly I was crying again. "I'm sorry," I said, "I think I
have taken all the Kleenex. I'm sorry to be such a baby."

The good doctor was very kind. He handed me his handkerchief, which I thought was a special mark of grace and
favor above and beyond the call of duty, an extra mark of
caring and concern.

He walked me to the door.

"Do you think I'm bright enough to find my way home?"
"Yes."

"Oh dear," I said, "oh dear, I hope so. I often don't know

225

enough to come in out of the rain and I seldom wear a coat even when it's cold. What's the matter with me?"

"Your authority-figure has fallen apart on you."

"Again? That happened all the time when I was little. I didn't know it could happen again when I grew up. Thank you for telling me. I'll send you back your handkerchief."

"Keep it," he said, "a memento mori for your illusions."

32

I DID get home alone all right. It was my first singular achievement. I went into the loo for a lovely long lifetime think. If I could not help Stanley with his problems because they were his own then I could and must do something about me. I looked at my face in the bathroom mirror, puffed and swollen eyelids were no solution. I put my head against the cooling tiles, recalling that day in England when I had come face to face with Edythe, Brandon's first abandoned wife. Not since then had I felt so caught in the middle, no place to turn to but the plumbing.

Plumbing is really very consoling. If you decide to cut your throat the blood can easily be washed away, if you decide to throw up it can be flushed away. Alas, I was not suicidal and alack, I am a stomach retentive, so thinking seemed the best.

My mind began to go round and round. If Helen and Brandon were not reliable, nor Simon, nor Stanley, if the marines were not going to land nor the cavalry ride up at the last moment, if there was no one anywhere to save me from the savage natives' attack then my illogical, logical conclusion left only one surviving fighter in the fort and the survivor was me.

Was it possible that all those strong and formidable warriors of my childhood fray were reduced by the light of psychiatry to less than life-size? They seemed very small at the moment.

In the nursery of the real world I was no longer sitting at the children's table, I was sitting at the head of the grown-ups' table. I was mother and if we were to have tea I would have to pour. What a panic to find I was the authority in charge. What a poor world Sarah could look forward to if I did not assume command rank because our officers had been killed in the field.

I cast about for a survival plan for Sarah and for me. The trouble with being breveted in the heat of battle was that I couldn't just stand there reading the rule book while the shot and shell exploded overhead. I had to assume command in an instant — just-add-bars-and-stripes sort of way and defend this indefensible position I happened to find myself in.

I put water to the face and looked at me again; no good to cry again, it would only spoil my actress face and gum up my sinus.

In this Tarrytown rumble I was outflanked, outnumbered, outgunned. My supply lines were cut, my communications severed, my command headquarters destroyed. If I stayed it was sure and certain death for me and my innocent child. I opted to run away to live to fight another day on some higher, drier, safer ground. The worst thing that could happen if I left was that Stanley would divorce me for abandoning ship. There, I had got the services and the wars mixed like apples and oranges and peas and potatoes, but I knew what I thought and I thought it was time to go even if there were a divorce.

Let me see if I could leave nicely, making a good clean exit, like making a good eighteenth-century death.

"Lovely Nursey," I said, "I must let you go."

"Why?"

"You are no longer needed."

"Who is to take care of baby?"

"Me," I said.

"Are you sure you are well enough?"

228

"Yes, I'm sure and I shall write you a reference tonight."

"Tonight?"

"Yes. You may go anytime."

"Mrs. Partridge hired me."

"And Mrs. Partridge is letting you go with two weeks' pay." There, that was done. I was shaking but it was done. I wished I were not such a coward. It would make being brave so much easier.

I needed a place to go to. I had a pang for the day when I could have rung up Simon and said, find me something. I did need help. No, that was bad thinking. I only needed an apartment and somewhere there was someone who wanted to get rid of an apartment and the *New York Times* was the very matchmaker to bring us together.

I ran my finger down the columns marked Apartments for Rent. There was one that would do, an artist going to Europe. A phone call to the artist, a bank reference to prove I was solvent and the apartment was mine; no need to see it, it had the proper number of rooms. I did not get a skylight but I did get something on a top floor and a lot of north light. Well, that was high ground, was it not?

I would have to work to maintain that bank balance. Could one call one's agent at home at this hour?

"Sorry to ring you at this time of night," I said. "It's Diana."

"What time of night, I haven't had dinner yet."

"Oh, the bliss of living in the town," I said, "no chickens to go to bed with."

"Cómo está? I'm switching from French to Spanish. The Spanish don't eat until late so what's by you?"

"By me it's moving time. I'm coming to live in the big city and I'm going to need work if I'm to pay the rent."

"How much is the rent?"

"Enough," I said, "can you get me enough work?"

"I can try. There aren't a lot of plays at the moment."

"Anything," I said, "the commercials, the soap opera, the stage, the cinema."

"I'll set up some appointments for soap commercials."

"Bless you. Take any ten per cent of me that appeals to you."

"We must keep this clean, amigo, and don't turn bawdy. Do you really need the money?"

"I'm the sole support of a hungry child."

"Oh. I'll do my best."

"How do you say 'you're the cat's meow' in Spanish?"

"I don't know. I haven't gotten that far yet. I can say you're the bee's knees, though."

"Say it to yourself five hundred times."

Well, there was shelter, there was possible food and now to clothing. I wished that I were not so grown-up that I had to rule out the possibility of stuffing everything into pillow-slips and cutting away within the hour. I don't know why but that was the saddest leave-taking bit of all, the paper cut that had the pain of the guillotine. If I did not pack neatly tonight there would be chaos to unpack tomorrow, cause and effect. Proper suitcases it had to be and lists and piles of clean clothes on the bed and checking to see what was forgotten and then keys to lock up the suitcases. What a world indeed to dread the possibility of thieves or to think a suitcase could ever be one's treasure or keys a way to keep it safe.

Sarah was my jewel and even she could not have safety guaranteed her in transit. I packed and sorted the night through and after the first light and the first coffee I went in and woke up Sarah and I said, "Guess what?"

And she said, "What?"

And I said, "We're going to the city to live," and she didn't say anything because she didn't know the city or very much of anything else, but that it was her time for breakfast.

"Where's Nursey?" Sarah asked while she drank her juice and ate her boiled egg.

"Gone," I said, "forever gone."

"Good," Sarah said.

"Didn't you like her?" I asked, surprised.

"I don't like a nurse," Sarah said, "I like a someone." I wished she wouldn't say my mind. I'd feel her chances were better.

"Was the egg all right?" I asked, suddenly insecure about my ability to mother her properly and wanting to change the subject.

"Yes," she said.

"Thank you," I said. One meal down and two to go today.

"What about tea?" Sarah said, "will we have tea in the city? I like teatime." I laughed.

"Yes," I said, "we'll have tea. Aren't you a funny girl to think of tea at breakfast?"

"I am," she said, "I'm a very, very funny girl."

And she was right. She was a very funny girl or we would never have survived that day. I was new to setting up a household and our apartment lacked odd supplies. Light bulbs and toothpaste and matches, things one took for granted had to be thought of and looked for in the shops. We did a lot of shopping and a lot of going up and down stairs.

I was inefficient and Sarah missed her nap but still we managed lamb chops for supper and baths before bed. Sarah went to sleep before I had her tucked in and I fell upon my bed too tired to sleep. There seemed to me something vital that had been forgotten, something that had to be done before I could rest.

It was Simon, of course. He was going and I must at least tell him where I was. He would need to know that in case of an emergency. I did not know what emergency I had in mind but he had to be told goodbye.

"Hello, Simon."

"Yes."

"I've left Mayerling. I'm out of the glass case."

"Oh?"

"I've got a new address."

"I'll write it down. Let me get a pencil." What a pang. Only acquaintances had to write down addresses. Friends always remembered. "I've got the pencil." I gave him the address. "How's the husband?"

"I don't know."

"I've read the papers."

"So have I. He's with his mother, Simon."

"Still in the glass case."

"In a way."

"Then you're alone."

"No, I have Sarah with me."

"Want me to come around and make you neat and tidy before I go?"

"No, I'm neat and tidy now. When do you leave?"

"End of the week."

"Then I won't see you again."

"Not unless you want to."

"I think not, Simon. I think I'll be busy unpacking while you're packing."

"I think I'd like to do something for you."

"I think that's a pretty thought and I thank you but there isn't anything to do."

"Then it's time to say goodbye."

"Time to say goodbye."

Long pause.

"Goodbye, have a nice trip, Simon."

"Goodbye, have a nice stay, Diana."

Now I could put me down to sleep and all the other things that had to be done could be done tomorrow and the day after and the day after that. I had a lot of time to get them all done.

Sarah was first on the list of things to be done.

"Listen," I said to her.

"I'm listening. Why do you ask me to listen?"

"Something important."

"What?"

"I have to go to work and you have to go to school."

"When?"

"As soon as we can find you a school."

"Let's go to the school today." I was surprised.

"Do you want to go to school?"

"Yes."

"Why?"

"I want children to play with and games to play. They have them in a school."

"How do you know?"

"Saw it on TV."

"Oh." I thought she might want to read and write. Well, maybe not. Anyway she had a mind of her own, that was something.

We found a school not too far away by the river. It was a church school, St. Wells, lots of red brick buildings but very human-looking for an institution.

Sarah went off with a teacher to look at a classroom and I went to see the headmaster.

"It's a lovely school," I said to the headmaster who was young and nervous and had a beard. I hoped he was qualified for his position.

"Is it?" he seemed startled. "I suppose it is. We're in debt," he said.

"Aren't you endowed?"

"Yes," he said, "but not enough. There's never quite enough."

"Do I have to be a church member to enroll a child here?"

"Good Lord, no," he said, bemused that I should ask, "most parents aren't. Do you want to know about the fees?"

"Are they high?"

"I don't think so until I try to collect. We can't do on less. We can't make do on this for long. We'll have to raise them next term, I'm afraid." I looked at the brochure he handed me. The fees were underlined in red ink.

"You teach French, I see, in the nursery school."

"Yes, in the playground. It's best to begin there, then it's all easy when they get to the upper school."

"What else do you teach them, faith, hope and charity? Do you teach them things like that?"

"Actually," he said, "that should read faith, hope and love, you know. Well yes, we teach them things like that. Things to recite before the milk, short things. Do you mind?"

"No, I don't mind," I said, "I just wanted to know."

"Well, really we learn more of that religious matter from them than the other way around."

"What?" I was agape.

"Prayer, for one," he said. "I've never been very good at praying, have you?"

"No," I said.

"They are," he said, "they pray for the essential and the absolute."

"Oh please," I said, "what is the essential, the absolute. I've always wanted to know."

"Oh, for hamsters not to die, and no more mumps and a whole family to go on an outing, things like that. Would you care to make out a check today? I'm so sorry to ask but we are rather pressed for money." I took out my checkbook and looked at my balance.

"Yes," I said, "I'll write you a check. I can just manage it."

So there was shelter and food and clothing and school and the greatest of these was Sarah's face, smiling.

234

"Do you think you'll like your school?" I asked her as we walked along home.

"I won't know till I've been there, will I?" She smiled.

"No, but what do you think?"

"I liked the pottery table. There's a lot of clay, you make it into shapes, put a glaze on and then you bake it and if it doesn't break it's something you can keep."

"Who told you that?"

"I saw it on TV."

33

I BEGAN to see me on TV which was a financial blessing. I saw me do the wash. I saw me do the dishes and I saw me on a soap opera as opposed to a soap commercial. I was in a car crash and then in traction in a hospital. They kept me there for days, an arm and a leg in the air. The pay was lovely and the work was nice. The lights were warm and the camera had one red, cheerful eye. I suffered very well.

I got much better at the housekeeping. I had a routine that was almost efficient and I began to enjoy the fun bits, the geraniums and the chives and wood fires. I bought a thermometer so I'd know what the weather was before I went out.

Sarah liked her school and she liked the someone that took care of her when I was working. She began to collect absolutely essential life objects; a marmalade-colored cat she found in an alley, two goldfish and a hamster that ran in a squeaky cage and annoyed the cat. She made an ashtray out of clay at school and glazed and baked it and brought it home without its falling apart. At least I thought it was an ashtray. She said it was a spoon holder. Well, each to his own point of view.

We each had a life of our own and one we shared. We both missed Stanley. We had a fiction for him. We said he was away on a trip and we stuck to our story which is why we were so surprised when he came to our door. He was the unexpected guest. He said he had come to take us out to dinner if we would care to go.

We said we would if he'd wait till we got our hats and our coats.

"How was your trip?" Sarah asked politely.

"Long," Stanley said and he looked at me. "Where shall we go for dinner?"

"You choose," Sarah said, "you asked us."

It was a pleasant restaurant, a pleasant dinner. Sarah and Stanley had a lot to say to each other. Stanley did not look very much better than when I had seen him last. He had been badly wounded in the wars. I was half surprised that he did not limp or use a cane.

We walked home after dinner, Sarah between us, holding our hands. She was getting tired. We sung her back and forth to divert her. It was good she had Stanley to carry her up the stairs. Stanley put her to bed and told her stories of the adventures he had had in faraway lands. He said he would take her to see them for herself one day and I hoped he would remember, for she would count it a promise.

I lit the fire and found a bottle of brandy and waited. Whatever he had come to say to me he would have to say for himself. I could not say it for him. Then he came and sat before the fire, tentative, testing the climate of the room, and it was very hard for him to begin and very hard for me to be patient.

"I've come in pursuit of you, Diana."

It was really unfair of him to begin with what I most wanted to hear. It took away all my resolve and left me fragile and exposed.

"I don't know why you'd want me and I haven't much to offer."

Did he want me to protest? How does one ever learn to fend off the blackjack-blows of emotional blackmail.

"I've left the Foundation." There was something I could answer.

"Is the inquiry over, then?"

"Yes. It was all a hoo-ha, a tempest in a teapot. I'm not to be sent to prison or even publicly censured."

"I never thought it was your fault."

"No, nor I, but still it was unpleasant and when it was over I wanted to tell them to go to hell so I did. I've always felt a stranger there, as if I had no real face, as if I didn't quite belong."

"Then you've done what you think best. There are other jobs."

"I hope that's true." Stanley reached out for more brandy. "I'm walking wounded."

I shook a little as I poured the brandy. Where had he got the expression? From me, I supposed, but it was so very much Simon that I felt some strange magic had been worked. Stanley took a great swallow of the brandy.

"I've left my mother's apartment." He really was enough to break my heart; no gingerbread man but a real man running from his dear old demon mother.

"I talked to Dr. Glass," I said. "He tried to explain about your mother. I didn't understand all of it but I think she's a real problem to you."

"I'm afraid so," Stanley said. "The thing that is so humiliating about it is that it's such an undignified complaint. I'm supposed to be an educated man, I've got a piece of paper that says cum laude to prove it. You'd think I'd never heard of Hamlet or the silver cord."

"Dr. Glass seems very nice," I said.

"That's what Dr. Glass said about you. He thinks you're very nice."

"Has he been a help?"

"Yes," Stanley said the yes slowly, "he has, but it takes

time, you know, to tear yourself up and put yourself together."

"Yes, I'm sure that must be so. But worth it maybe if there's someone there at the end."

"The real help," Stanley looked at me quickly and then away, "was Simon."

"Simon?" I repeated, stunned.

"He came," Stanley said, "one night right out of nowhere. He said he was going to Paris to live and he couldn't leave without seeing me."

"Simon?"

"Yes."

"He'd read the papers and he knew I was in a sling. He said he had been a friend of yours and wanted to know if there was anything he could do for me."

"Simon? I'm sorry to keep repeating that but I cannot imagine Simon coming to see you."

"I thought he was looking for you, but no, he said it was me he had come to see."

"And he said he had been my friend?"

"Yes." I had a pain for the past tense.

"Well," Stanley said, "what could I do? I asked him in and we began to talk. He's really a remarkable person."

"I know," I said.

"It was as if he were in my head and saying what I had never been able to say."

"What did Simon say to you?"

"He said that there are people who are bound to do their duty. I didn't see any sense in that at first because of course one must see one's duty and do it. But he said that was not always the noble or the good it seemed to be. That it was sometimes just being bound by a necessity to fill in a blank space in oneself. I couldn't see any blank space in me, certainly, and then I got to thinking about my father being out of the family picture and feeling as if I must be a hero forever got up in armor to save my mother from her distress.

"Simon said being bound by a duty like that was no better than being bound and gagged and held a prisoner in a castle. Simon said it was rather like being held a lifetime prisoner for an impossible ransom.

"He asked me what the first duty of every prisoner was and I said, 'Why, to escape,' and he said I must be my own escape committee. He said he knew I was wounded, maybe I had only one leg to stand on but my only hope was to make a crutch, stand up and hack my way out. He said he was in the next cell and had no legs at all but he said he'd keep talking to me until I got free."

I thought everything Stanley was telling me was a ridiculous parody of the Simon I knew. How could Stanley have reduced Simon to a story from *Boy's Life*.

"I didn't know," Stanley said, so earnest and so sincere that I wanted to weep over him, "if I could make it or not. I had a time of panic and I said to Simon, 'Where do I go if I escape?' and he said, 'Home.' Well, I want to come home. I got out of the dungeon if not out of the castle and I want to come home, Diana."

"Listen," I said, "I want you most terribly. I never change. I'm a very constant wife but I have a few bounds and lacks of my own."

"You have your work. Simon says that the stage is much the best for you. Simon says of the three of us you are the luckiest because of the work. I could take care of you, run your errands, wait for you at the stage door. I could be very useful."

"Like Mr. Margolies," I said, "taking care of Helen."

"Someone has to do that work," Stanley said. "It's a job someone has to do."

"I'm not a divinity," I said, "or a bright star. I'm just a working actress. I like the work and sometimes I need an agent or an accountant or a lawyer but none of those things are what I need from you."

"I don't know what I can do."

"Get a job of your own. Be my husband. It's time there was a wedding. It's time Iphigenia stopped feeling cut up by her mummy and daddy."

Stanley laughed. I had made a little joke and he had laughed a little. It was I who felt most serious.

"I need," I said, very, very carefully, so that Stanley would be sure to hear me, "I need a husband with a job and a father for my child." Stanley nodded.

"Simon says that if I found work to do that was more than a day-to-day job, something that I felt I could do better than anything else, that it would be like finding a fortune in the streets. Simon says that for people like us, working eight hours a day is never enough. Simon says that . . ."

"You can tell me the rest tomorrow," I said, "we must get to bed. I have an early rehearsal in the moring."

And that was true but most of all I wanted Stanley to stop telling me what Simon said. For I had a new despair. I did not know if Stanley would ever speak for himself and if he did not how would we all end?

EPILOGUE

EPILOGUE

34

IT is Christmas Eve in the morning. I sit propped up in bed drinking my morning coffee and trying to learn my lines for a new play that I am to be in. It is off-Broadway, not on, but I like the play and I like my part and I hope I'm going to be bloody marvelous. The money is not much but the soap opera goes on so I can afford to do something I choose.

The door to the bathroom is open. I can hear Stanley and Sarah chattering away at one of their early morning conversationals. He is shaving and she is sitting on the edge of the tub watching him as if he were about some sacred rite. He has been telling her something that happened at his office.

Stanley has a job. I am very pleased for him. He did look for a very long time before he found it. He was very discouraged and I yearned and yearned to make him stay at home warm and safe and never go out of doors to be rejected by the cruel world. But that would have been like his mum tending and taking care of him so I gritted my teeth and let him go. He likes the work. I think it's a bit early to tell but he seems to be coming along with it.

Sarah is telling Stanley about this afternoon's Christmas program at St. Wells. We are going to see her in a nativity tableau. She is to be a lamb and she says to look for her, she will be the one lying down by the third shepherd from the

245

left. In a rush of motherly solicitation I had asked her if she needed any help with her play.

"No," she said quite nicely, "do you need any help with yours?"

I do need help with mine. I believe this new play is an allegory, about the truth, the lie and the illusion and how human beings try to reconcile the three odds to make one even. Is it? Helen once said never worry about what a play means. You'll play it the same anyway.

"Listen," Sarah says to Stanley.

"I'm listening," he says.

"I have a question."

"Ask away."

"Mary is baby Jesus' mother. Right?"

"Right."

"Baby Jesus is the son of God. Right?"

"Right."

"Then who is this Joseph?" There is a long pause.

"He is," Stanley says, "the man who paid the taxes."

Perhaps my play is about identity and who we all are. Perhaps that's what the playwright is trying to say. Perhaps that's the message. Still, I must say the lines, best learn them first and worry about the meaning later.

"I thought," Sarah says, "that Joseph was that man with a lot of brothers and a crazy-quilt coat."

"That was another Joseph," Stanley says and he begins to whistle a Christmas carol.

"Oh," Sarah says.

We have a pretty Christmas tree, there are a lot of presents under it. We have a bird for the basting tomorrow and there are the three of us in a place of our own. That should make a Christmas. I hope it does.

I cannot remember the first Christmas I spent when I knew for certain sure that absolutely nobody was going to come down that chimney. I think this year is a little like that. Knowing does not alter the season. One can still have an expectation of joy.

Sarah and Stanley have been very busy wrapping and hiding and giggling over their presents for me.

"What do you want for Christmas?" they had asked. "You must make a list. We must know what you want." I made out the list. It was not a true or complete bill but it would make me content; no point in asking for the impossible or in trying to give impossible presents either.

Whenever I have had a moment off from rehearsals I have been Christmas shopping. I'm in a very wanting-to-give-everything-to-everyone mood this year. I would like to give Helen and Mr. Margolies two tickets out of their hiding. I would like to give Brandon his youth. I'd like to give Simon a loving heart. I'd like to give Stanley a soul to call his own. I'd like to give Sarah an unbreakable guarantee that she could fly away from us when she was able.

But I have been practical and settled for things I could find in the shops. For Helen I have found an enormous jigsaw puzzle that doesn't turn out to be anything but hearts and flowers. I'm also giving her a copy of *Stuart Little*, I'm sure she's never read it; for Mr. Margolies some penny plains and tuppence colored that he's been trying to find for ever so long; for Brandon and the wife and the babies things to blow up and put in the pool. They are plastic but nice. It will give them a group activity for Christmas in Hollywood.

I meant the gifts kindly. They are all children's presents for children who never grew anything but older. One can't stay angry with children even when they have turned you aside and pushed you away. They meant no harm, they were only thinking of themselves. Even under the law children cannot be punished as if they were adults.

For Stanley I have found the most marvelous leather coat. It's lined with fuzzy fur and is big enough for two or more; and also an ivory chess set. Perhaps he can teach me to play;

for Sarah lots of silly, very un-useful presents, bells and balls and balloons. I have also found her a book. I have had her name put on it. In it she may write anything she pleases and she will never have to open it to a living soul unless she wants to, for it has a key.

For Simon I found a yellow fish made of Japanese paper and hung from a golden thread. I thought it was so pretty that it might divert him. I wrote "Merry Christmas" on a yellow card and I wrapped it with great care and then in the end I could not send it, for I knew that Simon would not send me anything this year and that he would have nothing more to say to me.